By M.T. Bass

MURDER BY MUNCHAUSEN

BY

M.T. BASS

AN ELECTRON ALLEY PUBLICATION

MUDCAT FALLS, U.S.A.

Electron Alley Corporation
The Herald Building
732 Broadway Avenue
Lorain, OH 44052

Manufactured in the United States of America

Edited by Elizabeth N. Love (www.bee-edited.com)

ISBN 978-0-9833807-9-5 (Trade Paperback)
ISBN 978-1-946266-01-9 (Pocket Paperback)
ISBN 978-1-946266-00-2 (eBook)

www.mtbass.net

For Lightnin' S. Norton

The Three Laws

1. A civilian-owned and operated synthetic humanoid entity may not act in any manner so as to engage in or cause any harmful or offensive contact against a human being or, through inaction, allow a human being to come to harm.

2. A civilian-owned and operated synthetic humanoid entity must obey the directives and orders given it by human beings except in those instances where such directives and orders would conflict with the First Law.

3. A civilian-owned and operated synthetic humanoid entity may protect its own existence as long as such protection does not conflict with the First or Second Laws.

Federal Technology Administration Regulations

Obviously, crime pays, or there'd be no crime.

~G. Gordon Liddy

The Warehouse

The abandoned building in the Warehouse District was dark and cold. I didn't have glass on the AnSub, but we were picking up an RFI signature that was an eighty percent match to the A-VIN profile. My Smith & Wesson eM&P was out and humming in my hand, ready for me to take a shot. Behind us the SWAT team was spreading out into position to monitor our visual feed from outside so they wouldn't jam the ambient signals with their tac gear. We went passive on our glass as soon as we entered the building.

I looked over at EC, my partner, pressed against the far wall covering the left side of the industrial cavern, which was piled high with discarded junk—desks, chairs, pallets of boxed materials and strange hulking machines that no doubt once fabricated some kind of pieces-parts necessary for the stuff consumers once found they absolutely-positively could not live without in their daily drone lives—all collected from businesses that absolutely-positively no longer existed. The quiet was oppressive and haunting. We both strained for an aural clue to the location of our quarry, since the electronic intel was still too weak to pinpoint within the building.

We slowly wove around the junk, deeper and deeper into the room. I led. EC followed, constantly adjusting the ePD scanning app to search and map the room. I muted the tactical channels and stripped most of the data from my view to let him work the tech and comm. It's too distracting. I needed to maintain focus. I needed to be able to react.

This particular Android Subject apparently went off the rails and killed a luckless pedestrian on his way to a bodega for some iced tea or bottled water to quench his thirst. A one-in-a-million occurrence, but every so often it still happens. Anyone who believes technology is infallible is a fool. The incident didn't appear all that nefarious when first reported, but shortly thereafter the Atlas data stream went dark and patrol called our unit in. It quickly became obvious we were dealing with a malware hit, not a malfunction. The luckless pedestrian was actually not so luckless, being on what appeared to be the winning side of a particularly nasty termination suit with his ex, who we suspected had outsourced the final settlement to extra-judicial parties.

It might not make sense, but the beloved Media tags it "Murder by Munchausen." For a price, there are hackers out there who will reprogram a synthoid to do your dirty work. The bad news: no fingerprints or DNA left at the crime scene. The good news—at least for us—is that they're like missiles: once they hit their target, they're usually as harmless as empty brass. The trick is to get them before they melt down their core OS data, so you can get the unit into forensics for analysis and, hopefully, an arrest.

EC's scanner returned a hard ping. His quick double blink put his cross-hairs up on my lens and I followed his eye line to the northwest corner of the building. I swept my eyes up and down to acknowledge and we slowly headed in that direction. As we moved, the RF signal narrowed and confirmed bogey lock with a low growl in my ear buds. EC swung out from the left and unshouldered his shotgun. Good old-fashioned blast power often came in handy to buy some time. Like I said, *usually* they're harmless, but usually just ain't good enough odds for me.

My Smith & Wesson started flashing yellow in my glass. It took the data hand-off and started frequency ranging, seeking the optimal setting for its electro-magnetic pulse to take down the AnSub. We slowly and methodically cleared the warehouse, aisle by aisle, until we got to the very corner of the building where the android had parked itself, facing out the window towards the city lights. In sleep mode, I could see its right eye's red optic laser reflect off the window pane as it lazily pulsed. We spread out as quietly as we could with our weapons trained on the synthoid perp. EC pulled the restraining bolt from his webbing and held it up. If we could get it in without discharging our weapons, there was less chance of frying any lines of code that the forensics guys would whine on endlessly about.

I nodded. I had frequency lock on the droid's GMC—Gyro & Mobility Chip—and kept my weapon pointed at center mass. Precise aim isn't critical but improves effectiveness and tends to minimize collateral damage to nearby appliances. EC moved in swiftly and smoothly. Since they all, literally, have eyes in the back of their heads, there's just no sneaking up on a droid like you can a human, so the best thing is to get it over with as quickly as possible and hope their reaction protocol has not been tampered with to ignore the RFID chip in our cop badges.

EC was within arm's reach when I saw both eyeball scanning lasers reflect off the window pane as the droid came alive. It spun quickly and reached for EC's neck. I reacted instinctively and double-tapped the synthoid with my Smith & Wesson. It's like tasering a human and, since it's just a machine, there's some entertainment value in watching the spastic jerking of arms and legs as the control signals are scrambled then flatlined.

The AnSub collapsed in a heap. EC kneeled down to place the restraining bolt in the small of its back, then radioed SWAT to stand down. He pulled his Department-issued *Google Glass* off and wiped the sweat from his forehead with the back of his arm. He looked up and, catching his breath, sighed, "Thanks, Jake. He was going for my throat."

"All in a day's work," I answered, holstering my pistol. The droid's mechanical strength would have made short work of EC's windpipe. "Besides, I couldn't let him ruin that lovely singing voice of yours."

EC smiled.

I winked back.

He knew he couldn't carry a tune.

The Meat Market

Misbehaving synthetic humanoids don't go through the normal booking process, of course, but we still bring them in through the sally port at the precinct house to be logged into evidence and lockered up until the forensics guys can do their digital autopsies. The sheriff's deputies who run the jail are always glad to see us because it gives them a chance to make fun of the one group of regular cops who are even lower on the social pecking order of the station than they are.

"Well, well, well…If it ain't the Geek Squad, again," snickered Deputy Ernst, raising his voice to announce our arrival to his squad. Ernst was a hairy ape of a man perfectly well-suited physically to supervise the swing shift band of gorillas in the "Meat Market."

"Great to see you, again, Deputy," I said with extra maple syrup dripping from my words.

"Look, guys, it's the Dynamic Droid Duo." Ernst's troop started to gather around him. "Bringing in Suzie Sexbot for solicitation, again?"

I could hear EC grinding his teeth beside me in the squad car. It was the one case we would never live down and the grief we took over it bugged the living crap out of him. But, pervs come in all shapes and flavors. We don't pick 'em. "Come on, partner. Take it easy. At least we're still loved more than Internal Affairs—*I think.*"

EC hopped out of the car and rushed off to get a gurney.

I got out and opened the rear door on the squad car. I had taken to handcuffing the synthoids when we brought them in as a subtle way of mocking the Meat Market crew. Maybe it was too subtle, so I decided to put on a little show.

"You…have the right to remain silent…"

As I recited Miranda to the droid sprawled in the back seat, I pulled it halfway out of the car and deliberately slammed its head hard on the car door a few times.

"Watch your head, sir."

I pulled it the rest of the way out and tossed it on the concrete floor in a heap, then pulled out my baton and whipped it to full length.

"…If you cannot afford an attorney…"

I smacked the sprawled out replicant human in the small of its back and the back of its thighs as hard as I could, the slaps of baton metal against synthetic skin reverberating off the concrete block and tile of the sally port. The groans and sighs of the Meat Market apes accompanied my performance as they watched and heard me do what they only wished they could.

"…Do you understand these rights as I have explained them?"

EC returned pushing the gurney and smiling at my antics.

For good measure, I kicked the torso where ribs would be, then took a deep breath and turned to Ernst. "Sorry you had to see that, Deputy. But sometimes it feels good to get it all out."

I collapsed my baton. We lifted the synthoid up and dropped it hard on the gurney. As we pushed it slowly past the swing shift of the Meat Market, their eyes followed us out with a combination of shock, envy, and animal hunger twitching in their fat faces.

Murder by Munchausen

"Feels good. Yeah. Feels good," I muttered to myself, but purposely loud enough for them to hear.

EC worked hard to suppress a laugh. When we got to the elevator, he asked, "Was that really necessary?"

I thought for a moment. "Yeah. Yeah, it was. Sometimes you've got to feed the beast."

"But everyone knows I.A. cleared you of the worst."

"Doubt is a powerful force, my friend. Like gardens, rumors need fertilizing and reputations need weeding."

Down in the basement, we transferred custody of our evidence to Gus. I scribbled my name at the bottom of the form and slid the clipboard to EC.

"You got this?" I asked him.

"Maddie?"

I nodded.

"Yeah. Go on. Get out of here."

"Thanks, partner." I headed back to the elevator to go up to my old haunt in Robbery/Homicide, where the coffee would be hot and company might be, if not more inviting, at least more visually pleasing — if Maddie was, indeed, there.

Robbery/Homicide

"What? No donuts?" I asked no one and everyone as I loaded up a cup with coffee. Maddie's desk chair was empty, so I scanned the squad room for her.

"Well, well, well...look what the cat dragged in," Lt. Sands said as he sauntered over to the coffee pots from his office.

"Hey, boss. What's new?"

Sands shook his head as he set his official police department cup down to fill it. Our careers crossed paths in Robbery/Homicide—his on the way up, mine on the way down. After the *"Incident"* and the Internal Affairs investigation, he crafted my out into the Geek Squad, saving my pension and giving my idle hands something to do during what would otherwise be interminably long and empty hours of a forced retirement.

Sands held up his cup and we clinked in mock toast. He took a sip without ever taking his eyes off of me. "Maddie?"

I shrugged, then nodded. Sands knew the back story of how I took all the weight and kept my former partner's jacket clean.

"She's around," Sands said. "What's new down the alley?"

EC and I had our offices in an annex building literally down the alley from the precinct, reaffirming our status as outsiders. It bugged EC because it made him feel like an exile, but I was just as glad to be as far away as possible from the bureaucratic and political bull crap in the House. I'd had my fill of it in my career. "Murder by Munchausen. Hopefully, the forensics geeks will find the signature of the re-code man for us."

Sands nodded, then said, "We never did work a case together."

"No, Lieu. Never did."

"Shame. Maddie says you were good."

Still am." I winked, spying Maddie stepping off the elevator. You couldn't miss her red hair, even when it was pulled back in a pony-tail, though I preferred it when she let her natural curls free to flow down her shoulders. More of an off-duty thing for her. "Speak of the she-devil."

Sands smirked and shook his head. He knew. Saw it in my face, no doubt. He turned to go back to his office. "Good to see you, Jake."

"Yes, sir."

Sands stopped and scowled back over his shoulder. "Don't call me sir."

"Yes, sir." I cracked a smile.

Sands shook his head and walked back towards his office. He warned Maddie as they passed in the aisle between the desks, "You've got a visitor, detective."

Maddie stopped and looked over at me. She arrested the smile that started curling on her face for the benefit of the squad room and shook her head. She slowed her usual manic pace and took deliberately measured steps towards me. "Detective."

"Detective," I answered as politely and officiously as she had greeted me. I shuffled over to her desk. "How is your day going today?"

Maddie exhaled a long, heavy sigh.

"There, there. Tell Jake all about it."

"Nothing to tell. Just the usual."

"Ah, humanity at its best being bad."

"Something like that. So what brings you out of the Alley?"

"Drop off for forensics."

"Another disorderly droid in public?"

"Actually, murder this time."

"Oh, *do tell*. It sounds positively marvelous."

"Well, no…nothing like what you *real* cops see every day." I scanned the crime scene thumbnails spread out on her *iSlate* screen. "That looks like a nasty one."

"Hooker in an alley—a *real* alley. Messy business. Completely unnecessary, but…"

"Yeah, I can see." I tapped the screen to open the gallery and swiped nonchalantly through the pics, then zoomed in on a body shot. There was something familiar about the mutilation of the body. "Hmmm."

"What?"

"Ah, nothing. What have you got to go on?"

"Zip. Zero. Nada. The scene was as clean as a whistle with regards to the perp. Too clean. Three days now and the case is starting to stink like fish and unwanted house guests. I really don't want it to go cold."

"Hmmm."

"You don't think a droid…"

"Nah, too vicious. Too animal," I mumbled, shuffling the pictures back and forth. It was gruesome, but there seemed to be a signature there. "Unless…"

I'd have to check my library of paper books, but there was something in the messy crime scene I had seen before.

"Dinner?" I asked.

"Yeah…I don't think so," Maddie did the *Price is Right* product arm swing toward her desk. "Gotta lotta work to do."

"Sure."

"But…"

"The door will be open. I'll be up late. I've got some research to do."

"About what?"

"I don't know, yet. Something caught my eye."

"You're the best. We could use any help we can get."

"Sure thing." I smiled looking forward to later, but wondering what it was I saw that was so familiar in that crime scene.

~~~

Old School

"There's Pinot open on the counter," I called out when I heard the front door to my flat open and close.

Good, I thought to myself, assuming Maddie got out of the House early. But then the clink of bottles as the refrigerator opened and closed told me it wasn't her.

"You don't mind, right?" EC asked as he sauntered into the living room holding up a Shiner Bock beer. "Holy calamari, what's going on in here?"

I had open books spread out and blanketing the sofa, love seat, leather lounge chair, and coffee table, spilling off onto the surrounding floor. "Research."

"Whatsamatta, the net down or did you forget to pay your bill again?"

I shrugged. "You can't think outside the box when you're locked in the box."

"That's what I love about you, Jake. You're so *old school*." EC shook his head. "I half expected to catch you watching *Ren and Stimpy* or *Pee-Wee's Playhouse.*"

"Ah, the classics…but, no, Maddie hates 'em."

"I'm not interrupting anything, am I?" EC looked around for Maddie.

"Nah, late night. She's still on the job trying to crack a hard nut of a case."

"And is that what this is all about?"

I nodded, looking around at all the mess of open books. I had a pretty extensive library of dead trees. People scoff, but predictive AI searches always lead you to predictable places. Noticing my wine glass was empty, I stood up and stretched out my back muscles. "Yeah. I thought I saw something in the crime pics in the murder book. Something odd about it. Something you can't put into words, so how do you Google it?"

EC followed me into the kitchen. *Do tell. I love a mystery.*

"Classic hooker in the alley scenario. The mutilation got my attention." I poured myself a healthy portion of Pinot Noir. "Something about the way the intestines were thrown over the shoulder and wrapped around the neck like a scarf."

"You've got an eye for details. Always have."

"It's a blessing and a curse." I took a sip of wine, then leaned on the island in the kitchen across from EC. "So, what brings you out slumming?"

"Got any snacks? I'm famished."

"What am I, your butler? Check the pantry. You know where everything is. Might be some nuts or chips or something."

"Guess I'm still wired from taking down that AnSub. It felt good. And, you know, a real case."

"Yeah. It did." I watched EC dig around my cupboards. He pulled out a bag of pretzels and tried one. He gave me a look that told me they were long beyond stale, then tossed the bag into the trash and dug deeper into the pantry. "Still too soon?"

"Huh? What?" EC asked coming up with an unopened bag of Famous Amos chocolate chip cookies. "These go good with beer, right?"

"I like 'em. Evidently, it's an acquired taste, though. Or so I've been told repeatedly by a certain female detective."

"What the hell." He popped a cookie in his mouth and washed it down with a gulp of Shiner. "So, the hooker? The intestines?"

"Puzzle pieces. You know. And there was a nice neat 'Y' incision, so it wasn't just an unschooled gutting out of rage."

EC popped in another cookie and crunched it up.

"I thought I might find something in the library."

"You do have an awesome collection."

I sighed and sipped my wine. "There's just something about ink on a page that can't be replaced or replicated with pixels."

"But nothing, huh?"

I shrugged my shoulders, mentally leafing through the volumes I had pulled down from the shelves in my study.

"I just didn't want to go home, yet, you know," EC finally confessed. "You and I, we had a good day and I didn't want that to go away yet."

I nodded. EC lost Pattie, his wife, in a car wreck back in January. "Yeah, it was something, wasn't it. I thought for sure the droid was going to rip your Adam's apple out."

EC chuckled. "It was a stroke of luck nailing him in that warehouse, huh?"

I popped a cookie in my mouth, grabbed the bottle of Pinot, and sat down at the kitchen table.

EC brought the bag of cookies over and we replayed the case and the capture from the top, so he wouldn't have to go home just yet.

~~~

Maddie

After I found the sediment in a second bottle of wine and EC had put a dent into the second half of a twelve pack, he headed back to his empty split-level in the 'burbs and I ended up in the leather lounge chair staring aimlessly at crime photos from the last century, flipping pages one way and back the other without focus, lost in inebriated thoughts of murder and Munchausen, EC's friendship and loneliness, a promising law enforcement career gone south, and rebounding into very different kind of partnership with my ex-partner.

The next thing I knew, I woke naked in bed beside her, trying to solve the mystery of just when she had finally gotten to my apartment. All I could remember was sleepily padding after her as she led me to the bedroom. A dream, perchance, but no. No dream. There I was spooning against her, feeling her warmth and her steady breathing against my chest.

I came up from nuzzling into her neck and noticed Maddie's shield and department-issued service weapon on the nightstand. I always found the Glock to be a rather soulless firearm. It never spoke to me like a 1911 or Colt *Python*. All they do is work, coldly and efficiently, but I suppose in the rather corporeal world where we spend our days cold, soulless and efficient is what you really want when your life is on the line.

Then it struck me.

"Jake?" Her voice was morning hoarse. "Don't."

"Huh? I—"

She grabbed my arm draped across her chest and held me to her. "Stay."

"Okay." But in my mind, I was trying to remember where in the puzzle pieces scattered on the furniture and floor the book was with the crime scene photo that had floated to my consciousness.

"I'm sorry I was so late. Sometimes I get a bit obsessed."

I tightened my embrace.

Maddie sighed heavily. "You know…"

"Shhhh." Never spoken of and only ever acknowledged in intimate moments like then, there is a toll your soul pays with every homicide you work.

No one wanted to work with Maddie when she was assigned to the precinct. It wasn't chauvinism. There were plenty of women in the squad already. But it was more than the discomfort of a change in the familiar routine or the extra burden of showing a newbie the ropes added to the weight of the daily grind of crime solving. Or even the jealousy of watching a thoroughbred fast-tracking her way to a command slot. Nope. Maddie was young and beautiful and, of course, a redhead, with all the usual attendant baggage and a smart mouth to boot. No one—not even some of the female detectives that walk that way—wanted to ride with that temptation every day.

Stupid me tempted fate, though that wasn't why I found myself at the other end of the alley on the Geek Squad.

Maddie's phone rang and she instinctively groaned. The ringtone identified it as the station house. She answered it and "uh-huh-ed" her way through the call. I knew the days off we had planned together were toast.

"Another one," she sighed wearily after she hung up.

I held her for the briefest of moments, then she rose to leave me.

~~~

John's Diner

The best buttermilk pancakes ever in a tsunami of maple syrup. Hard, crisp bacon and a huge glass of milk. That and about a gallon of coffee helped shake the sediment of Pinot grapes out of my brain. I wondered, briefly, how EC was doing. He was pounding down the Shiners pretty hard.

I passively let the sugar and caffeine work their magic on my biologics, gazing blankly out the window at the mid-morning traffic on Detroit Avenue. No crime books. The *iSlate* dark. Just me and breakfast. At some point, I'd have to decide what to do with my two days off, since my previous plans with Maddie had been overcome by events. But I didn't have to decide just then.

"So, where's Red?" Amy asked coyly, sliding onto the booth bench across from me and slapping her paper waitress order pad down on the table. *John's* is old school, too. Amy, though, is twenty-something. She slowly pulled an undone strand of blonde hair back off her face. "Flying solo?"

Her tone was a little too perky and a little too pregnant with expectations. Those days were over, though. At least for now. "Murder and mayhem in the big city. You know how it goes."

"Yeah, Jake. I do know how it goes." Amy cracked an alluringly half-crooked smile.

I smiled back. Temptation abounds. Just then, my phone started vibrating on the table. I looked at the screen. It was Maddie.

Amy scowled and grabbed her pad. She leaned over the table as she stood up. "I get off at the usual time…"

I watched her pirouette and sashay towards the kitchen.

"Hey," I answered Maddie's call.

"Hey. Got a quick minute and wanted to call. You know, sorry and all about having to rush off this morning." Her jaw was locked unsmiling in crime scene mode. I saw frustration in her eyes.

"Duty calls. I get it." Not every mate did. It's one of the advantages of keeping it in the family. "All day pass?"

"Well, if forensics ever moved faster than a snail's pace," Maddie said loudly, turning to direct her comments over her shoulder at the crew in bunny suits working the scene behind her. Then back to me, "I could get myself sprung maybe in time before the Fire Escape Grill closes?"

The fire escape in question was the one on the back of my building and the grill, my charcoal Weber. Old school. "I'll talk to the proprietor and have him keep the kitchen open."

"Thanks, Jake. I need it."

"The usual?"

"Yes, please." She paused, looked off screen to her left, and listened. I ignored the muffled voice and followed Amy with my eyes as she carried an order from the kitchen to a table. "Sorry. Gotta go."

I nodded. "Okay."

The screen went dark.

Hadn't planned on grocery shopping on my day off, but what the hell. I decided to go by the West Side Market. And I'd probably have to pick up all the crime books strewn about the place. No doubt a mood killer for Maddie after a hard day at the office. Great. More domestic chores. But not yet.

I tossed a generous tip on the table and grabbed my stuff. As I passed by on my way to the register, I put my hand on the small of Amy's back, feeling her young muscles clench in a familiar way.

"Try to stay out of trouble, you," I said lowly into her ear.

"Is that personal advice...*or professional?*"

"I'm just a cop on the beat, ma'am."

"Stop by anytime, officer."

I paid my bill and left.

~~~

The Fourth Estate

"So…where's your partner?" the inquiring reporter ambushed as I stepped out of John's Diner.

With the wisps of warm memories of Amy's body still dissipating in my mind, I reflexively responded by guardedly asking myself, *Which partner?*

"Ah…*yeah*…I meant EC." He had no doubt caught the warmly confused look on my face. "I know from the Atlas scan app that Maddie's on the job."

"Are you stalking me now?"

"Slow news day."

"No, it's not. It never is. How long?"

"Oh, 'bout half a short stack."

"Asshole. Why didn't you come in?"

"Professional courtesy? Maybe? Didn't know if you were on duty or not since you were solo and—*so, who's the blonde?*"

I followed his eye line into the diner to Amy who was waving at us. I waved back. "Put a sock on it, ya mook. She could be half your age."

"Yeah, but a man can still dream, can't he?"

I kept those thoughts to myself.

Jamal was an indie but a good one. He mainly did tech stuff, but he had found a niche for himself in my little corner of the world where electrons collide with corpuscles on the wrong side of the law that kept his byline—E.J. Quick, probably his maiden name—on millions of screens on an all too regular basis. He swears he created the whole Murder by Munchhausen tag. He's probably right, but I'd never let on that I thought so—or that I even read his stuff, which I did. It was more fratricidal ego hazing than professional discourtesy. Jamal was a good guy. I liked him.

"That was a nice catch on the droid."

"It's why the city pays me the big bucks."

"So, spill. Got the data dump yet?"

I rolled my eyes. "As if…"

"Come on. The vic was Judge Mullaney's third-second cousin or something. Right?"

"Damn Irish. Kill one and they all take offense. Anyway, you know the lab squidlies in forensics. Their clock speeds ain't exactly set to the Naval Observatory."

"But you'll let your favorite journalist know as soon as the results come in."

"Journalist? You flatter yourself."

"Hey, let me get a pic—so my editor knows I'm not just sitting around in my pajamas making stuff up." Jamal spun and pressed himself to my side, holding out his phone to take a selfie with me. "Is that a pistol? Or are you just glad to see me?"

"Did you at least get my good side?"

"Jake, you don't have a good side."

~~~

Edgewater

When I've got nowhere to be, there's no place better than being at the lake. Also, public parks are nearly exclusively occupied by humans. Synthoids don't need R&R, so the few there to pick up trash are uniformed in Metroparks logoed jumpsuits and are easy to avoid.

So, I hoofed it back from *John's* to the building that I "inherited" from Mom and Pop, where my apartment was above what used to be their shop. My sister took it over, but couldn't clean up the mess left behind after probate and I bailed the building out of IRS purgatory with a chunk of my settlement stash. It was okay between us. I had no interest in a flower shop and Karen made an honest go of it, but her heart really wasn't into floral arrangements either. So, no hard feelings.

But now, the shop was a big empty man cave for my play things. I rolled the Indian *Chief Dark Horse* out the garage door that led to the alley out back. It's my preferred mode of travel since motorcycles don't have a "Rochester" chauffeur mode—and I *hate* putting my life in the hands of self-driving cars.

I cranked the engine and headed down to Edgewater to hang and watch the waves crash. The sound aurally scrubbed my mind, clearing my thoughts. Funny, how not thinking can help you think.

I sat for a long while on the rocks, then wandered the beach, which was mostly abandoned in the middle of the week—at least 'til the day was pushing noon, when the people watching got a little more interesting as folks started gathering like lint and hair in a drain trap. You can never turn it off completely, even when you're off duty. Always making judgments and sizing up intents, whether it be ill or otherwise. An involved couple meeting to share a sandwich. A scattering of businessmen brown-bagging it to seek out a little serenity in the middle of the work day. Teens who should be in school but weren't, with no ill intent except to escape the educational warehousing for a day. The ones that always draw closer scrutiny are those who sit in their cars, especially on a warm, sunny day. Their visages are always the least social, rarely smiling, staring like hungry panthers at prey. My eye is immediately drawn to the license plate number. Like I said, you can't turn it off.

But I was off duty, so I walked back, then east out around the marina and the power plant to Whiskey Island. Pumping my legs helped the thought process a lot, too. Somehow, I solved many a tough case wandering aimlessly about the city. There was nothing really to noodle over on my case with EC—at least until the forensics guys finished up analyzing the synthoid's hardware, firmware, and software. We had the AnSub; we just needed the accomplice who programmed the murder and the perp who paid for it. But Maddie's case was still festering in my mind, chewing on my gray matter like the waves gnawing and eroding the shoreline.

I got back to the water's edge on the north side of the island and mindlessly watched an ore boat breech the break wall to head upriver to deliver its mined goods.

"Another one," Maddie said when she got the call from the House that morning.

Murder by Munchausen

I didn't need to see those photos to know what that meant and the look on her face when she called from the crime scene confirmed it: the same person had committed both murders. It was early, but no doubt the thought had already put down roots in the back of her mind that she may have just caught a serial murder case…and that brings a whole new set of calculations into the equation. Some of it is bureaucratic and procedural and exceedingly annoying—like when do you actually invite the brass to start looking over your shoulder with a microscope at every little thing that you do and when do the federal frat boys at the F.B.I. crash the party and then the whole public relations nightmare with the media. I don't mind sparring one-on-one with Jamal and his ilk, but standing in front of a pack of hungry news cameras and microphones to feed their pathological need for attention? In a way, it is its own Media by Munchausen. No thanks. Been there. Done that. Been second, third and fourth guessed by every expert out there with their own blog and by-line. But, come to think about it, Maddie would probably look great and sound smart streaming onto all the big screens at the end of the media pipeline. She might like it. Me? Not so much.

On the other hand, the hunter in us all can't help but feel the adrenalin rush of being on the trail of "big game." Hell, it's not even my case, but I got a mainline dose of it just looking at the crime photos. Homicides are usually just messy and emotional, no mystery or matching wits with a mastermind. You're essentially cleaning up the temper tantrum of a toddler armed with a deadly weapon. But it's a completely different ball game when the act of taking a life becomes some sick mode of self-expression. And unlike the unsolved cases that can take their toll over time with their lack of answers, a serial case eats you alive because you're not looking back asking 'why.' You know there is a new victim coming, so you're looking ahead and asking 'who' and 'when,' feeling powerless to stop what you know will happen.

I knew Maddie's mind had already started going there, wondering about the third vic.

So, while the hunter in me yearned to join the pack, the lover in me wanted her out. But I knew that would never happen. This was the kind of case careers are made out of…and she knew it, too.

I walked back to my bike with selfish thoughts swirling unverbalized in the back of my head and disrupting any professional attempt to connect dots into a usable and meaningful pattern.

~~~

The West Side Market

Mel, the Butcher, saw me coming and waved his cleaver at me. I waved back and slowly meandered down the crowded aisle of the open market, mentally taking note of the produce and bakery offerings along the way to his stall.

"The usual?" asked Mel as I stepped up to his counter.

"Yeah. A couple of Freddies, please." Mel didn't know who Fred Flintstone was, but he knew that—whoever he was—he liked his steaks extra thick. I watched him saw off a couple of cowboy rib steaks that would barely fit on the Weber. I mentally drifted back to the butchery in the alley.

"You got a big case?" Mel asked in his thick Slavic accent, noticing my faraway look. "You look like you got a big case."

"Me? No. No big cases for me anymore." I shook my head. "Maddie, though…"

"How is Miss Madeline?"

I sighed out loud.

"Jake, Jake, Jake…" Mel shook his head and wagged his butcher knife at me. "Don't screw this one up, too. She's a good lady."

Maddie and I used to stop at the West Side Market for gyros when we were just work partners and wander up and down the aisles scoping out the food items, since we both share a passion for good eating. You wouldn't think that a career woman cop would be such a good cook, but she knew her way around the kitchen. I found that out later, during my suspension, when she came by to cheer me up with plateful after plateful of gourmet goodies. Truth be told, I'm just an animal flesh searer. She's the one with the culinary artistry. Mel knew the same thing from her interrogation of him on different cuts of meat, like she was wringing a felony confession out of the butcher.

"Yeah, I know. I know. That's what everybody tells me."

"Well, then, you should listen to everybody then. *Huh.*"

"Just throw those Freddies over this way."

The steaks landed with a satisfying thud on the counter top, like a heavyweight boxer hitting the canvas. I smiled and slipped Mel bank scrip for the meat—more than they weighed out to—that I'm sure went right into his pocket. The government tried hard to take the cash out of society, but that just ain't how people are in the real world.

"You listen to everybody, my friend. *Listen.*"

"Sure, Mel. Sure."

I saluted and wandered on down the aisle, listening instead to the voice inside my head and doing my people-perp watch of the crowd.

I missed it more than I admitted—at least to the outside world—being a people cop, I mean. I guess the Poindexters EC and I go after are people. Barely. Not exactly the usual stuff of crime statistics, anyway. Just not much sport in it really, just digital ones and zeros for evidence, mainly, and a geeky computer nerd at the end of the trail. Maybe that's why I latched onto Maddie's case so quickly, but I didn't really believe that. Just playing *iPsych* on myself—something that I got too much of a taste of from the Department shrinks.

Murder by Munchausen

I mean, just being so close to a real flesh and bloody crime investigation, I could feel the heat of passion, anger, ambition and a tinge of fear, like standing close to a radiator. Truth be told, it's a pretty intoxicating cocktail. But the bottom line is that there is somebody doing bad things to people…very bad things that have to be stopped. And there was something there in the crime pictures that I saw but didn't yet see.

The faces in the Market dissolved into a blank, fleshy canvas as I sliced through the crowd like a shark through a school of tuna.

And I'm sure my eyes looked just as cold and empty to the schooling shoppers.

~~~

The Fire Escape Grill

Unconsciously, I sorted the books scattered around the loft into two piles as I tidied up the place for Maddie. I had thoughts of running the vacuum, but, well, I got sidetracked by black-and-white eight-by-tens from a hundred years ago or more. I re-shelved the bigger stack of books and towered the other off in an out-of-the-way corner, hopefully where it would stay out of Maddie's eye line. I surveyed the joint. The place was clean enough. I just had to ensure footprints weren't left in the dust and that all other possible work-related distractions were properly tucked away out of sight.

I went out to preload the Weber and Frank the Feral Cat was there waiting for me with an impatient look on his face, so first I took care of his needs. He followed me into the kitchen to keep an eye on me like the wary feline that he is. I took his tuna back out to the fire escape and he eyeballed me as I dumped charcoal into the stovepipe starter and stuffed it with scrap paper from the precinct. As he settled into wolfing down his meal, I sat down on the fire escape and dangled my legs over the edge with a beer, soaking in the long summer sun. In the winter, with the trees stripped of their leaves, I can just barely make out the lake through the cuts between the houses and apartment buildings. Once spring comes, it's gone, so I watched the traffic and the birds and the occasional pedestrian as I waited, slowly and methodically stripping my mind of thoughts like old paint off of woodwork.

"Hey, Jakie," Maddie called out what could have been minutes or hours later or maybe even days.

"Out back!" I answered.

A few minutes later, she climbed out on the fire escape with her lawn chair and a glass of red wine. She plopped down and took a long sip. "Hey, Frank."

Frank acknowledged her arrival with a long, impatient look up from his tuna.

"Oh, my God. That sun feels great," Maddie exclaimed. "Bring it on. Bring it on."

"Hungry?"

"Mmmm…I will be."

"Mel says 'hi' and that I should pay attention more—to you, that is."

"Yeah? Maybe you should take his advice"

I looked back at her over my shoulder.

She smiled wearily.

I wasn't going to be the one to bring it up.

"Exact same M.O." Maddie sighed heavily. "Definitely dealing with a sick puppy."

I nodded. I understood completely.

"You got anything?"

"A gut feeling."

Maddie nodded. She understood that if you force it, like a bird in the bush, you flush it and maybe never see it again.

"I—"

"Later. We've got all night." I got up and took her hand to lead her inside to the bedroom.

Murder by Munchausen

She didn't resist.

After, we lay naked for a long while, not speaking, then I got up and lit the grill. I watched the sunset.

Maddie appeared behind me, dressed only in a tank top and a pair of short shorts. Her hard, well-exercised and well-tended body teased beneath the thin fabric. Her hair waterfalled down across her shoulders like I like it. She sipped at the glass of wine she had poured when she first arrived and admired the setting sun. She sighed contentedly.

"Yeah."

"Yeah."

We don't call it the Fire *Escape* Grill for nothing.

Eventually, the coals glowed orange hot and I started searing the cattle flesh. Maddie went in to rattle around the kitchen to prep our side dish. We sat in our lawn chairs in the dusk at the end of the daylight, eating our steaks and talking about sports, work politics, city politics and what we should do on our vacation together in the fall—everything except the five-hundred-pound gorilla of a subject in the room—until we ran out of ways to avoid it, so we went to bed to wrestle more tenderly this time and fell asleep.

"Sands says he'll hold off going to the brass," Maddie said when we met at the coffee pot the next morning as she made her way to the shower. "But if it starts getting too much play in the media…"

"He'll have no choice," I finished her sentence. "Obviously."

"Yeah. Managementspeak."

"Got anything?"

"Precious little, except the profession of the victims and the eviscerations. The Bunny Boys picked up some DNA material, but with the revolving door on their panties, who knows where that will lead."

"Well, start practicing your media doublespeak."

Maddie rolled her eyes and took a sip of coffee. "What about your Munchhausen Murder? Anything back from the Wonder Kids?"

"Oh, I imagine Q will have something for us this morning. I'm just glad EC has the patience to endure his techno-babble. I sure don't."

"Always at the mercy of technicians," Maddie whined sympathetically.

"Press '3' for all the ways that technology has not made your life better…"

We dressed and armed ourselves for the work day, then went our separate ways.

~~~

The Grease Monkeys

The first stop EC and I made was the back room in our building known as Mechanical where the grease monkeys tear down apprehended synthoids in a half-assed autopsy. Bob and Puff were hunched over our droid bickering like the old married couple they practically were. EC cleared his throat.

"Hey there, guys," Bob said in his sing-song way, standing upright and wiping fluid off his hands with an oily rag. He was the rounder and jollier of the two. Puff, tall, lean and curmudgeonly, just grunted and kept poking around the wires and tubes in the torso through the abdominal access panel.

"Spring a leak?" I asked, pointing at Bob's hands.

"Yeah, you know, boy, it's a funny thing…" Bob smiled and chuckled, adjusting the glasses on his face. "Some of the bio-hydraulic lines in the legs and rib cage were ruptured. Nasty take down, I guess. Huh?"

Puff stood up straight, bringing some kind of electronic module from inside the droid to the tip of his nose to examine, squinting at it to bring its label into focus. "The *Dermal-Lite* on the back of the thighs had lateral impact impressions…like from a baton." He squinted my way. "You wouldn't know anything about that, would you?"

I shrugged innocently.

Puff looked at EC, catching his smirking half-smile, then

grunted and dove back into the guts of the synthoid. "Right. *Idiots.*"

"So what's the story on this unit?" EC asked.

"Well, I'll tell ya, guys," Bob wound himself up with a deep breath, "it's a standard Omega Gen-3 chassis, but there's definitely been some special modifications."

"Chop-shopped?"

"Yeah, yeah, yeah—but these guys aren't hacks. They seem to know their way around bio-robotics pretty well. And they didn't use cheap gray market replacement parts. All OEM stuff, but they mixed and matched from the Big Three. Look here, a Fanuc Dexterity Control Unit," Bob pointed into the abdomen of the synthoid, "mated to a Mitsu BLC. And over here's a GD mobility module." Bob shook his head. "I don't know how they got their hands on a military grade mobility pack."

"But the Gen-3s aren't as vertically integrated as the earlier designs, right?" EC asked.

"True. True," Bob's bald head bobbed up and down. "And swapping out subassemblies is a pretty effective way to get around the embedded RSHA protocols to defeat the Three Laws."

"Yeah, so, they're all Frankensteins to one degree or another, right?" I asked.

"True. True. You can't do it all with just software. But this one—"

"The mobility module," Puff said curtly. He stood up again, twirling what looked like a hip ball and socket assembly in his hands. He squinted one eye shut towards EC and I. The stare down seemed to last forever.

"He's right, you know," Bob finally interrupted. "That's the wild card."

"How so?"

"Generals need to know where the grunts are, but not the enemy," Puff explained without elucidating the matter.

"Yup. Army synthoids aren't permanently latched to the Atlas grid like civilian units," Bob said. "Otherwise, troop movements could be seen by the bad guys. I couldn't begin to tell you how they hacked into a mil spec GMC, but this is definitely post graduate work—maybe even Ph.D. level."

"Post hole diggers?" I asked to lighten the mood.

Puff glared at me.

"Did you get the black boxes pulled?" EC asked quickly before another staring contest got under way.

"First thing we did, fellas," Bob answered. "Got them over to Q yesterday morning."

"Great. Thanks, guys." EC headed towards the door.

I took a last long look at the tangled innards of the murder weapon. I looked over at Puff. "Serious, huh?"

He ran his fingers through the thick shock of his graying hair. "As a heart attack."

I nodded and followed EC out.

Puff's squinting eyes tracked me the whole way out the door.

~~~

Q

EC planted himself at his desk and began mining his inbox for word back from the code analysts. I sat down and pulled a pad of paper out of my desk to start my daily "To Do" list. Old school. But scrawling out my hopes and dreams in long hand was always more effective for me than doing it online and stuffing them into a cloud somewhere—who knows where. Out of sight, out of mind—and people wonder why nothing ever gets done.

Our Elba was called "Exit Alley," back behind the precinct building in an abandoned warehouse that the city foreclosed on and put forth a minimal effort to renovate in order to get us out of the hair of the "real" cops. It drove EC crazy. I was just as glad to be off the chain of command's immediate radar—especially now with the cold shadow of a possible serial killer hanging over their heads. Maddie's case would ratchet the tension in the squad room up for everybody.

Our "offices" were nothing more than a big open bullpen with desks and a few file cabinets. We did have a couple of conference rooms/interrogation rooms along the side wall that got more use out of HR and their endless training sessions, than they did wringing confessions out of reluctant perps. Usually by the time we apprehended a hacker, their will to resist—usually as weak to begin with as their upper body strength—had evaporated. There were four other officers exiled to the Geek Squad. Two of them had actually requested the duty, having come up through IT, white collar crimes, and forensic accounting. None of them had seen the street in their entire crime fighting careers like me and EC. They hung out with Q and his gang on their breaks—*as if…*

"Bingo! Q's got something for us," EC exclaimed and I watched his lips flap as he read the email from our resident forensic programming genius and reverse hacker. Q had some kind of shady past that was never mentioned by anyone in the squad and that tickled my interest not one bit, *or byte,* depending upon your technical orientation. EC hopped to his feet. "Come on, Jake. He says it's something we need to see for ourselves."

I made a show of lumbering reluctantly to my feet and shuffled after EC. The Brainiacs were in another part of the warehouse, in offices much nicer and more climate-controlled than ours, which boiled in the summer and froze in the winter. Thank you, Mr. Mayor.

Q's world was one of cubicles and the quiet tap-tap-tapping of keyboards, like a constant depressing rain against a windowpane. He greeted us at the door and motioned us into a severe white conference room with modern white furniture. You almost had to shield your eyes from the glare. The pale green paint somebody viciously picked for our decor was already peeling, even though our side had been renovated at the same time as the lab's. EC and I sat on one side of the table. Q sat across from us and pulled out a printed out report on…*more white paper!* How could the Brainiacs sit in such brightness all day long and not get even a hint of a tan?

I sat back in my chair. EC leaned in to listen intently to Q. That wasn't really his name. I tagged him with it because I refused to engage lab rats on a personal level. Evidently, he actually knew who James Bond was and even Ian Fleming—one point in his favor—and took a shine to his new nickname, so it stuck. He was also able to affect a scruffy unshaven look, being one of the few males in the colony who could actually sprout whiskers, so he didn't look fourteen. Another point. And if I was being completely truthful, he had a gritty attitude about rules that I found appealing—but I never let on.

"We've found some recurring subroutines and library links in the coding that are *very* interesting." Q laid out sheets of paper filled with typed gibberish cascading across the page. His index finger darted into different lines of code like peccadilloes until it finally stuck on one line of code highlighted in yellow. "And this call out here is particularly intriguing."

That's odd, I caught myself wondering. *Q? Paper?*

"And why is that?" EC asked with interest.

"Well…" Q shuffled more papers in a file folder and pulled out another couple of sheets. "It is an external call out into a cloud bank that has, well, evaporated."

Techno mumbo jumbo, I thought. "Okay…"

"It is obviously a ploy to keep forensic evidence out of the synthoid's firmware by putting it where it wouldn't be found or would be destroyed after the mission was concluded."

"How would they do that?"

"It might be triggered by an event, like the crime, or time deadline or even sensor input, like a spike off the RFIDs in a cop badge." Q scratched his whiskered cheek loudly. "It's a new twist. Actually, quite creative."

"Well, where is this cloud bank?" EC asked.

"And that, gentlemen, that is the funny thing…" He folded his hands on top of the papers and stared first at EC, then me.

"What?" I asked impatiently, but not from Q's transparent attempt to build suspense. My spider senses started tingling at 'quite creative.'

"Commercial services are required by the Public Utilities Commission to keep LUDs—*Local Usage Details*—on cloud account activities, which can be subpoenaed."

"So, we need to get you a subpoena?" EC's voice betrayed reluctance at the prospect of official paperwork.

"Well, I would say yes, if I thought it would lead us somewhere useful. But I already know that it would be a dead end."

"And how do you know that?" I asked.

Q rolled his eyes and feigned a Spanish accent, "'Cause we don't need no stinking subpoenas here."

"At least not unless we want it to be admissible," EC noted impatiently. Q was even starting to irritate my partner.

"But there's no sense in wasting all that time and judicial goodwill when we know there won't be anything useful to be *admissible.*"

"And we know this how?" I asked again, a bit more sternly.

Q stared back at me. "I've read the I.A. transcripts on your...*incident*—"

"Those are sealed," I said. "Or are supposed to be."

"Yes. *Quite.*"

"So?"

"Then you do understand." Q swept up the pages of printed out code. He tapped the edges square on the table and slid them into the file folder. He reached to his belt and pulled off his Android *Alpha-Bit* and placed it on the table between us like an ante in a poker game.

"That's not department-issue," EC noted.

"So, report me." Q stood up and motioned silently towards the door. "You in or out."

EC and I pulled the *iNodes* from our belts and anted up. As far as the Atlas grid was concerned, we'd still be sitting in the conference room with Q.

Q rounded the table and headed out.

EC and I looked at each other, stood up, and followed him out of the conference room and down the hall, offices on the left and a cubicle farm on the right.

When Q got to the end of the hall, he pulled out a burner and tapped swiftly on the screen, then silenced the alarm on the emergency exit and held the door open for us. We all went out into the alley that separated us from the precinct house. Q produced a flat piece of hard plastic from nowhere like a magician, slid it between the latch and the jam, then pushed the door shut behind us. He squinted up at the security camera to make sure its blinking red light was out. He gave us a smirk.

"Lovely aroma," EC said, sniffing the air and eyeballing the dumpster.

"What can I say? My gang loves Indian food," said Q.

"So, the cloak and dagger routine…for why?" I asked.

"*For why,* because the LUD breadcrumbs lead back to the NSA. And Samantha noticed in her pattern analysis that the logic loops therein are, shall we say, bureaucratically bloated and inefficient."

"Samantha?" EC asked.

"You'd like her. She's cute." Q winked.

"NSA?" I asked.

"A lazy copy and paste job. It appears to be a routine to access metadata."

"But why? How did a domestic dispute gone awry end up in a hack into the NSA?" I wondered out loud.

"Hey. Me, I'm forensics. Remember?" Q asked pointing his finger into his own sternum. Then he wagged his long, skinny index finger between EC and me. "You are the detectives. So, detect."

"Okay, so email me your findings," EC said.

"Uh-uh." Q shook his head and handed EC the thick manila file folder. "Breadcrumbs. I don't want any knocks on my door—personally or professionally."

EC and I looked at one another.

Q pulled the emergency exit door open and stepped back inside. "You guys coming back in?"

"Nah. I think I need some air—fresh air," I said, looking up at the security camera. "I think we're gonna take a walk."

"Suit yourselves." Q pulled out his burner. "I'll give you a minute or two to clear the alley before I turn big brother back on. This gonna take long?"

I looked at EC. He shrugged. "Give us an hour."

"Excellent. Since I'm off the grid, I've got some errands to run." Q smiled cryptically. "Ping me once and I'll clear you back in to adjourn our meeting and get your *iNodes.*"

Q slipped back into the building.

EC and I headed down the alley to *Cutty's Deli,* where we knew we'd be away from prying eyes and ears…*and lenses.*

I looked back over my shoulder at the security camera and saw the red light come back on.

~~~

Cutty

Cutty was a retired cop who developed an expertise in deli meats during his twenty-five years on patrol as well as some pretty strong opinions on the proper assembly of a great sandwich and the improper pollution of coffee with anything other than real dairy cream and real sugar from real sugar cane. His place was always busy, even though it was around the corner and tucked away from the Justice Center. It was a place where plea deals got made, because prosecutors and public defenders checked their indignation as well as the Bill of Rights at the door and where cops spoke freely and frankly about the facts—admissible and otherwise—of their cases clear of the mist and fog of Department policy and political correctness. Although there was no sign on the door, the place was always completely devoid of politicians, both civilian and those wearing blue. Oh yeah, and no one from Internal Affairs—past or present—ever showed their face there. Evidently, Cutty had some history with them, too. Most of the good ones do—or so I'd been told by Cutty. He was my training officer went I first got out of the academy.

EC and I got a booth in the back and it wasn't long before the ex-cop appeared at our table dressed in a stained white apron.

"Howdy, boys." Cutty swirled amber liquid in a department mug that had never been stained by coffee—at the precinct or in its afterlife at the deli—and took a sip. His affinity for Scots Whiskey was well known. "The chili is a particularly good batch today."

"Are you kidding me?" EC snickered. "I've got to ride with this guy for the next five days."

"I'll do it. Make it a five-way," I said to Cutty, pushing away my unopened menu, then scowled across the table at my partner. "EPA and EC be damned."

"That's the spirit."

"Then give me a pastrami Reuben," EC countered. "With slaw."

"Nice. Fighting fire with fire. It's going to be an aromatic tour."

I shrugged my shoulders.

EC smirked.

"I heard you scooped up the droid that iced the judge's son. Nice work." Cutty winked. "But…what about the Geppetto pulling the strings?"

"Funny you should ask." EC tapped the envelope from Q with the forensics report. "Appears to be complications."

"Always are…Always are."

"Yeah, but these might be of the *federale* variety," I sighed.

"Ouch. Sorry to hear it. No one needs that." Cutty paused to peer at me over his mug. After another sip, he grinned and added, "Just ask Maddie in a week or two. How's that case working out for her? Word is that she'll be surrounded by pressed suits and starched white shirts before too long."

"Don't get jealous now, Jake," EC teased.

"Actually, I feel sorry for the suits. She has a knack for getting her way. Trust me. I know."

"You've always played with fire," Cutty said.

"I'm not the only one with third-degree burns on his soul."

"Yeah, but most people wait for the afterlife." Cutty winked. "I'll put in your order."

We watched him head back behind the counter.

"So, what do you think about Q's report?" EC asked when Cutty was out of earshot.

"A breadcrumb."

"You want to follow it? Knowing where it could lead?" EC sighed heavily. "I ain't got the energy to be sparring with DC's boys—especially if they're spooks."

I pondered for a moment. "I wonder what it really means. You heard Q. Anybody can hack into anyone's short hairs if they want. Why would this guy want? It's a local judge. A local crime. No need to go all *Mission Improbable* about it. Maybe, like Q said, he's just a lazy cut-and-paste kind of guy."

"Cutting and pasting from the NSA? That's a special kind of lazy."

"Inside or outside. That's the question."

"I hope it's outside. You know there's no way we'll get any help from the Company minions." EC arranged and rearranged his silverware.

"Depends upon what he was tapping into and why. Maybe, just maybe, the worker bees don't want the ruling class to know there's air leaking out of their tires."

"And just who would you talk to about that?"

I tapped my chin with my index finger. "Hmmm. I might know a guy who knows a guy."

"Yeah, well, I don't want to know."

Cutty returned with our lunches. *"Bon appétit."*

EC and I traded evil smiles as we prepared to load up our intestines with ammo.

~~~

The Federales

EC went back to the precinct to retrieve our iNodes and start data mining known associates of the victim and his spouse to prep for our interview. I headed down to Lakeside, then took a right over to East 9th and sat on a park bench across the street from the Federal Building. I took out my latest burner phone and dialed a number inside.

"Yeah, can I get a pizza to go with no anchovies?" I got the response I expected from the familiar voice inside and pocketed my phone. *Secret Service, my ass.* That place had more holes in it than the Pacific Fleet after December 7th.

The engineers and programmers do a good job and most people can't tell the mechanical droids from the human drones on the street even at a reasonably close distance. More likely, though, is that they just stopped paying attention, like ignoring regular people in the crowd every day. If you know what you're looking for, though, you can spot them easy enough. Of course, after the last year or so, I'm a bit more tuned into them, like a fisherman reading the surface of the lake for a school of walleye. They're still digital creatures, not analogue like us humans, so their movements are just a bit too crisp and hard-edged, even from a distance, mostly at the knees and elbows. Of course, it's even more obvious when you come face-to-face with one. Too many muscles in the human head, including the big, fat one between the ears. But it's getting harder, though, because the industry is always getting better, especially with the new active plasma biologic materials they are developing. And research showed that people react subconsciously to rhythms of bodies around them, so the Gen-3s even mimic the diaphragm movements of breathing and have nano-motors to generate pulses in the neck and wrists.

What struck me most, though, as I observed the activities on the plaza across the street, was just how many synthoids there were wandering around the Federal Building. I started making mental notes, as was my habit, and eventually noticed the same droids circulating randomly around the plaza. *Ah…security droids.* No doubt the first line of defense in any attack against the government. I wondered what my Secret Service pal thought about his job description being automated.

Eventually, my "pizza" got delivered.

"J-man," muttered the tall, dark-suited civil servant as he wandered by my bench. His eyes were shielded by government issued Ray-Bans. He stopped at the East 9th Street crosswalk and looked up at the traffic camera perched above the signal lights.

I stood up and meandered to the corner, then crossed Lakeside against the light. Cloak and dagger crap. A bit overly dramatic, but a small price to pay.

Eventually, we crossed paths again at Short Vincent Street and headed down Superior Avenue to the library. If you knew where to go, there were still dark holes deep, deep in the stacks, safe from prying eyes. Nineteenth Century literature was an appropriately dim corner of our modern day Orwellian reality.

"You off grid?" He hissed between his glowing gritted teeth. He still had his sunglasses on, like the cheesy Federal LEO that he was.

I nodded.

"Good. So, how's tricks?"

"Can't complain." I shrugged off the question.

"Yeah, well, I could, but where would it get me?"

"Maybe promoted to a GL-9?"

"Funny, Jake. Real funny."

"Yeah, I'm a riot. That's what I.A. put in their report. So, now I've got *that* on my permanent record."

"So, how can I help you today, Citizen?"

"I don't know. Maybe I can help you."

"How so?"

"How about spook code infecting my murder investigation?"

"Huh. Homeland Security? Insecure? Imagine that. Is this that judge's kid?"

I nodded.

"Interesting…"

"Ya think?"

"No. Not really." He sighed heavily. "Do you know how many lines of code it takes for the federal government to rule the plebes?"

I shook my head. "Or wait. Is this a joke?"

"Sadly, no. Nobody does. And that's the problem."

"I'll bet it's gotta be at least as voluminous as the tax code."

"Yeah, well, at least the private sector is anal about their magic pixie dust."

"Capitalism. You gotta love it."

"You'd think, but…You know the only real competition in

civil service is in the area of mudslinging and backstabbing."

"I thought the NSA was a cut above anyway—especially on mudslinging. You know, the new J. Edgars, the ones with brontobyte-sized files on everybody, born and yet unborn, and the total lack of fear or ethics to use them to protect themselves and their own dark wants and desires."

"NSA? Well, that's different. Those guys are bad ass."

"So again I ask, why is their code polluting my crime scene?"

"And how do you know this?"

"Really? You want my source?" I feigned outrage since I knew he knew.

"Q, right?"

"He's good. At least that's what EC tells me. And he is actually pretty effective when he's not in one of his moods."

"I'm surprised he doesn't work for them."

"Him? The NSA? Never." I shook my head and fingered the bindings of books on the shelf. "Q wouldn't be caught dead working for *The Man*."

He answered with a Federal-sized grunt of indignation. "You got something for me?"

I took out the page with the code that Q highlighted. "Don't get any Inspector General types involved, okay? I just want to know if this guy is inside or outside of government."

The *Federale* snatched the page out of my hands and skimmed over it. "Jesus. How can anyone stare at this crap every day, all day, and not go mad."

"And not go mad? I think you answered your own question. Q is anything but even-keeled."

He nodded, folded the page back up and stuck it in his suit jacket. It was actually nice that not everyone in government dressed like a golf pro. "I don't know where this will lead, but you understand that I'm not sticking my neck out too far on this."

"Of course."

"But I'll chum the waters and see what kind of carp comes to the surface."

"Carp or crap?"

"Neither one is good eating, so what's the diff?" He pulled down a volume from the shelf. "Read much, Jake?"

I nodded.

"You would." He smirked and showed me the cover: *Frankenstein* by Mary Shelly.

"I'm more of a fan of her husband."

"Who's that?"

"Never mind. Let me know if you hear something." I started to turn to head out of the stacks.

"Hey, hey, hey—what about me? You know how this works: *Quid pro quo.*"

"What do you want?"

"I don't know…*something.*"

I had to stop and think, really think about selling out Maddie and whether it was worth it, but nah. Sure, he'd score points giving the local F.B.I. guys two floors down a heads-up on a serial killer case coming their way, but it's Maddie and I hate to admit it: I am sweet on her. *And,* I hate bureaucratic backscratching—it's unsightly like the simian grooming on Monkey Island at the zoo; but, ugly as it is, it's the way of the world. Of course, there had yet to be any *quo to quid.* Besides, he owed me from last time, so by my scorekeeping, I was still ahead.

"I might have something juicy for you, but not yet."

"What?"

"Don't worry. It'll be good." I turned and headed out of the stacks, calling back over my shoulder, "Though actual mileage may vary."

~~~

Mrs. Victim

Now that we had the murder weapon and we were starting to get some leads on the reprogrammer, it was time to chat with the judge's daughter-in-law and, from what EC found in his search, he hinted she might be a doozie.

We made a good Mutt and Jeff team. EC liked doing his homework and researching the hell out of an interview. I preferred to be more of a blank canvas so that my impressions weren't colored by information already smeared on my psyche. It's important to get a clean read on a person of interest, and if you're painting-by-numbers, sometimes staying inside the lines takes your eye off the big picture. EC got it. So did Maddie—at least when we were professional partners. It's not so easy now. But, you know, things always change.

The Widow Mullaney agreed to see us in their penthouse apartment a couple of blocks down the hill from the bodega where her husband was programmed out of existence. After our formal introductions, EC sat down across the coffee table from her and took out his *iSlate*. Laying it on the table, he hit 'Record' and pulled up his research notes.

I drifted over to the huge picture window that looked out over the mouth of the river from the east bank. Out on the lake, an ore boat hovered near the break wall, waiting for a railroad drawbridge to rise.

I closed my eyes and listened to her voice answer EC's basic opening who-what-where-when questions—like a polygrapher trying to get a baseline reading. Her voice was smooth and calm, yet her thoughts were carried forward with a strong undercurrent of authority, like a doctor who actually deals with patients on a regular basis—and effectively, too, though she would probably be a nightmare to the nursing staff.

"So, did you and your husband have any registered Personal Services Assistants?" EC asked, going down his list of questions like a head coach calling in the next play in the game plan to the quarterback.

I turned from the window to put a face with the voice in time to see her shake her head in a measured way that didn't ripple or disturb her straight, shoulder-length blonde hair.

"Of course, the building has several in service for maintenance, housekeeping and, obviously, to patrol the parking garage, but we had no call for a PSA for ourselves," she answered coolly and evenly.

Her face was cut in a sharp kind of way that matched her voice, giving her beauty a hard, perhaps dangerous, edge. It held an expressionless cast as she spoke, like an eight-by-ten glossy promo shot or an ID badge portrait. She looked up at me with hard blue eyes. I smiled but got no ping back.

"What about work?"

"The usual orderly duty droids at the Clinic. I believe my husband's law office had them for library retrievals and returns. Typical stuff. Nothing very high-level. I am a geneticist. We don't do surgical or office procedures, just basic patient management and movement functions. I prefer human staff in my office."

Right, because getting up in a droid's grill isn't nearly as satisfying as

Murder by Munchausen

berating a fellow human being, I thought to myself. Synthoids are all programmed to take so-called "Droid Rage" completely passively, which doesn't really work too well in being an emotional pressure relief valve for the human. Though every once in a while it makes for fairly entertaining watching when a registration holder decides to post a vid-log of someone who totally loses it with technology. It's good there's no such thing as assault and battery on inanimate objects—they're basically indestructible to a barehanded human anyway—but it does give one in my line of work pause when you imagine that kind of rage precipitating a domestic abuse call or murder scene. And some people wonder why we still carry guns.

As EC continued on with his questions and Mrs. Victim responded with her emotionally flat-lined answers, I surveyed the room and noted a discernible lack of testosterone in the ambiance.

"So, your husband wasn't living here anymore, right?" I interrupted.

She broke engagement from EC and looked up at me.

EC knew what I was doing and watched her like a hawk.

I smiled.

She smiled back with the slightest crack of her lips. "Why would you say that?"

I shrugged and did a panoramic sweep of the room. "I just get that kind of vibe."

"Vibe?"

"Yeah, you know, we're guys. We still mark our territory like the animals we are. Sometimes it's an 'I Love Me' wall or display case. Other times more subtle: trophies from our life's adventures…and conquests scattered about."

Her brow furrowed for the first time during our interview.

"I don't sense it. Not in this room, anyway." In reality, the building's doorman had tipped us off.

Behind the glossy mask, her gears were turning so hard you could practically hear them grinding like a first generation robot.

I smiled.

She finally broke and smiled back with the smallest of shoulder shrugs. "It wasn't something that we wanted out there for public consumption, even with family."

"A rough patch? Or something more serious?" EC probed gently.

Mrs. Victim sighed and finally the needles moved. "I think Alec might have overreacted a bit, but…"

"You?" I tried but couldn't keep all of the accusatory tone out of my voice.

She nodded.

Her hard professional demeanor slipped noticeably, but I wasn't sure if it was just part of her disarming bedside manner act. "Attorneys?"

She nodded.

Of course, EC had already found that out from the scuttlebutt at Cutty's, though no paperwork had been filed yet with the court.

"We don't have to tell you how these dots lay out on the page, do we?" EC pressed a bit. "It just happens all too often."

She looked back to EC, more guarded now.

"Prenup, I presume?" I asked.

"Of course."

"Another dot, then."

"I see." Her voice turned icy, so much so I swear I could see her breath. "Well, then, I suppose I should talk to that lawyer of mine about these dots you seem intent upon connecting."

"Now, Missus Mullaney—" EC tried to calm the waves.

"That is *Doctor* Mullaney," she scolded, then stood up.

EC sighed, then stood up.

I shoved my hands deep into my pockets and took a last look about the penthouse.

"I think we are finished here." She addressed us curtly as if we were hospital staff.

"Yeah…for now." My eyes tracked back to hers. No more smiles.

EC swept up his *iSlate* and we left the Mullaney apartment.

"I'll bet she's a hell of a good doctor," EC said on the elevator ride down.

"Scare the sick right out of you," I agreed.

Prime Time

"Uh-oh," EC muttered through gritted teeth as he spied the news vans from channels three, five, eight and nineteen parked haphazardly out front like they were fire trucks and the precinct house was ablaze. Instead of hoses, axes and water cannons, cameramen wrestled with cameras, microphones and anchorettes-in-waiting. We cut down to St. Clair and came around back. For once, I bet, he was glad to be exiled down the alley. I wondered if Maddie might be wishing the same thing by the end of the day, but I doubted it.

We don't have a lobby or a desk sergeant, just a cubed off entryway with a couple of intentionally uncomfortable chairs. In one, Jamal sat smiling like a loon.

"Look EC, a reporter," I said in a hushed, reverent voice as if I had spotted an extinct spotted owl. "You hardly ever see one around here."

"Yeah. It's kind of like finding honesty at City Hall," Jamal snickered.

EC grunted. He waved his badge over the keypad to unlock the door and went inside, leaving me alone with "the Press."

"So, whatsamatta? Didn't you get invited to the really big show?" I teased.

"Since when did any truly useful information ever get

released or exposed at a *really big show?* It's just a kabuki dance for the cameras."

"And that brings you here? For why?"

"So, how's Maddie handling it?"

"Don't know—and probably won't 'til later. Haven't seen her since we went on duty."

"Well, you tell her that if she ever needs a friendly ear to talk to…"

I rolled my eyes.

"Yeah, well…"

"Seriously. You are here, *for why?*"

"You know that Sands and PR weren't going to take any questions from me, so what's the point? I can replay the stream and get what I need from the talking heads at my leisure—with a strong drink in my hand—and then I'll have the exact same info everybody else has without standing around pathetically begging for scraps."

"And being the crusading pursuer of truth, justice and the American way that you are…"

"Actually, I came across an interesting tidbit about Mister and Missus Mullaney that I, oh, I don't know, thought might have some currency on the information meat market."

"Oh, well, then, step into my office." Instead of sweeping my badge over the keypad, I held open the door out to the alley.

Jamal threw out his lower lip in an exaggerated pout.

"Trust me, you don't want to go in there." I shook my head. "Come on, I'll buy you a cup of coffee."

"And a danish?"

"And a danish," I sighed wearily.

Murder by Munchausen

With the press vans out front, the food trucks parked around back. Even so, they probably did a better trade, what with the rush of blue soon to be scurrying out to stay off camera. I bought Jamal his low-fat latte and a bear claw. I got black coffee. We wandered to the back corner of the fenced-off parking lot and sat on the hood of a patrol car.

"Good luck," the reporter said, surprisingly sincere.

"With what?"

"Prime time."

"How's that?"

"Oh, I don't know. This kind of thing can swell a gal's head, what with all the attention and notoriety. I'll bet she'll look great on camera—not like you."

"So you're saying I should be worried?"

"You tell me."

I thought about it for a minute. "Maddie's definitely on her way up the food chain, but in her heart and soul, she's a cop, not a suit. It's in the family DNA."

Jamal nodded and gnawed at his pastry. "But..."

"But what?"

"That incident down in The Flats."

"What about it? I was cleared. *Officially.*"

"Sort of."

"Yeah. So?"

"How discreet are you guys—you and Maddie? You know that my intrepid colleagues will spare no drop of rare and precious journalistic sweat to dig up dirt to juice their ratings and page views. And you, my friend, are dirt. Internal Affairs may have cleared you, but they didn't clean you up any."

"Hmmm."

"I know you can take it. What about Maddie? Especially, if there's not a quick arrest and the investigation starts to drag on. It's good to be the hero. Not so much being the goat day in and day out—especially when bodies are piling up."

"I guess we'll see, huh? She's a good detective."

"Those ain't the skills she'll need for this."

I took a loud sip of coffee.

"Anyway, good luck."

I shrugged. Truth be told, Jamal's reporting on the incident precipitating my suspension was fair. Not necessarily pretty, but fair.

"You know that the judge's son was not such a nice guy. With his family connections on the bench, he had things pretty well stacked up against his soon-to-be ex. She doesn't have much juice outside the Clinic."

"Yeah, we picked up on that right from the start."

"Did you also pick up on his extra-curricular marital activities?"

"Ah, no. Do tell."

. "I believe it kind of fouled up his lawyer's play with the pre-nup," Jamal smiled. "They did a good job of keeping it under wraps for a while, but it's not something the judge can sweep under the rug. Unless…"

"Unless the missus was wading in the same waters."

Jamal shrugged. "I hear that some of the women were, shall we say, hourly workers."

I nodded. "So he had needs, needs that maybe his hygienic and antiseptic obsessed wife did not care to indulge in. It happens."

"Sure, but here's where it gets interesting: Maddie's second victim."

Murder by Munchausen

"Oh no…" I froze in mid-java sip.

"Oh…*yeah.*" Jamal polished off his bear claw, licked his fingers and took a huge gulp of his latte. "I don't think it will come up today in the presser. Not likely anyone even knows yet. You didn't. *Does Maddie?*"

I lied with a shrug of my shoulders.

"But, rest assured, eventually someone's going to step off the sidewalk and into the gutter with me on this one."

"And how did you come to have this tasty morsel?"

Jamal put his shocked face on. "Do I ask you for the recipe to your Cajun rub?"

"Fair enough. But what are you going to do with that info?"

"Well…I just don't know yet. I'm working on a story, but the timing has to be right. If I release it right now, it will get lost in the thundering hooves of the media stampede heading Maddie's way right…about…now." Jamal looked over at the precinct building. A tide of uniformed officers ebbed out the back door towards the food trucks. He chuckled to himself. "Oh what a tangled web we weave…"

"…when first we practice to believe." I hid my concern over Jamal's information behind my coffee cup.

"Well, right now, it's actually just a thread that needs to be pulled a bit more. We've got to stay ahead of those pancaked-faced Bozos and Bozettes to find out what it means."

"What do you mean 'we,' Kemo Sabe?"

"You don't think this information is of value to you personally, as well as professionally."

I nodded slowly. It was—or would be.

"Just remember who's your pal." Jamal pulled out his phone and surfed to the stream of the press conference going on inside the precinct house. He held the phone up so I could see the screen. "You want to watch?"

I shook my head. I'd hear about it later. First hand.

Jamal smiled. "And you thought the geek squad was going to be low profile. *Sucker.*"

I looked at Maddie answering a question. She looked good, even on the small screen.

"When was the last time a camera crew came down the alley to your offices?"

"Well, let me think—like never."

"Yeah, well, good luck with that." Jamal looked at his phone. "She looks good. You're a lucky guy. You'll need it."

"Good luck with what? The press? Or Maddie?"

"Both, my friend." Jamal hopped down off the hood of the squad car and sauntered off. "Thanks for the bear claw."

~~~

The Flats

I sat in the dim twilight of the dying day on my sofa, staring at the stack of books in the corner that deserved a serious second look—especially now with Jamal's G2—to compare to the crime scene shots of Maddie's now infamous "film at eleven" worthy murders. Before, my interest in her case was a personal, say, curiosity. Now EC and I were going to get sucked into the media wave like into a rip tide. I hesitated before diving in.

The case that brought so much grief into my life was, of course, political. Maddie and I had "inherited" it because the Captain wanted to put fresh eyes on a high profile murder, after consuming so much time and department resources with so little results. We had been on a streak and just put away a butcher, a baker, and a candlestick shaker in short order, after they had killed a wife, a lover, and the last one a rival by smashing in his head with—wait for it—a candlestick, respectively and in that order. Instead of the gratitude of the city, we got a case that stank like the garbage truck servicing all the downtown restaurants.

Dr. Mullaney's apartment overlooked the Flats—the industrial lowlands around the river stitching its way up from the lake like a nasty knife wound that has always been the cultural equivalent of the Chilean Triple Junction, where commerce, crime and the creatures of *haute couture* have long collided for fun and profit. Amazingly, one of the dinosaurs from the Industrial Revolution times still spits out steel, fed by the ore boats off the lake. The rest lay abandoned. One has been turned into a hydroponic vegetable hothouse and tilapia farm, but the stink of industrial agriculture isn't much better, just different. On the West Bank, establishments cater openly to the baser needs of the city's citizens: liquor, drugs and women. Safely separated by the river, the East Bank is home to condo boards and gourmet cuisine that is really just a facade to the well-heeled's pursuit of the same baser needs. Crime, like magma, oozes between the cultural tectonic plates into the streets and alleys on both banks of the river. Most times it gets left alone, until blood is spilled.

Maddie's pedigree hearkened to the East Bank. I'm more a West Bank Joe—more *Harbor Inn* than *Ritz-Carlton*. Maybe that's why the Captain gave us the case. He knew I'd bulldog my way through the bull crap, but that Maddie would keep me on a short enough leash not to pee on the wrong hydrants. The best laid plans…

I just remember sitting in the interrogation room after I shot the Councilman's son as the weight of the city's political machine just began to bear down on me. I could feel Maddie's presence on the other side of the glass. It was almost telepathic, but we were always connected that way somehow. I could hear in my head the counterpoint of her thoughts, cursing me and thanking me for going into the parking garage alone and coming back out with four fewer bullets in my Glock. The Councilman's son deserved it. It was a good shoot, but, still, he was a Councilman's son. Hell, the Councilman deserved it, himself, being as dirty as he was, but that wasn't our case. We just needed to find out what happened to Sara Ann. And we did. Unfortunately, I scorched my career in Robbery/Homicide in the process.

It was ironic, then, that my current case centered on the East Bank luxury condo of a judge's wife and Maddie's victims were West Bank working girls. And now, again, we'd be going down into that circle of hell known as The Flats. Only this time we did not ride as partners.

I needed to do my homework. So first I watched a replay of Maddie's press conference in the growing dark, then flipped on a light and cracked the books.

~~~

Partners

"Did you see?" Maddie blurted out the first thing when she got to my place that night. She was uncharacteristically bubbly. "How'd I look?"

I looked up from my book. "Mmmm…a little too, um, formal for me. I prefer your Casual Friday Night look."

"Yeah. I had to go out at lunch to buy this stupid thing." She looked herself up and down in the dark pinstripe pantsuit, then shook her head. "I gotta get out of this monkey suit."

"You did good," I called out after her as she went into the bedroom to change. I meant it. She handled the press like a trainer holding the leash at the Westminster Dog Show. But that wouldn't last long. And like an overbred AKC pedigree, media types have a mean streak lurking in their DNA: MDS—*Media Derangement Syndrome.* "What did the brass think?"

"The weasel from downtown said I need to work on tightening up my answers to questions."

"Corporate is never happy with what anyone does outside their building."

"But Sands and the Captain were pleased. At least Sands said so."

Lt. Sands was a standup guy, but the Captain weather vaned freely with the political winds. That's how he got there. "Good."

Maddie came back barefoot and dressed in only a classic Joe Montana *Forty-Niners* jersey three sizes too big for her. He was making a big comeback in the NFL. Robots don't get concussions, but after the initial battle bot novelty wore off, the League realized that they needed on-field personalities to keep the fans engaged, so they started mining the Hall of Fame to give their rosters some soul. She carried a couple of wine glasses filled with a red of some sort and offered one to me. We clinked and drank, then she nested in against me on the sofa. She softly hummed a tune I didn't recognize as she sipped again.

I knew I had to tell her what Jamal told me. I also knew it would dampen her mood—to say the least. Hell, I wasn't happy about it. Working a case is hard enough without complications and entangling a serial spree with another high profile murder vic was definitely a complication—for me as well as Maddie. I didn't have to imagine how she would take it. Partners know. But I had to tell her…eventually. Right time. Right place. And now didn't seem to be the right time, until she forced my hand.

Maddie's gaze eventually settled on the stack of books in the corner like dust in a moonbeam. She stopped humming and sipped. She was thinking about her case. I knew I had better get it over with because waiting would only make it worse.

"The press came to see me today, too."

"Yeah? What did Jamal want? Did he need you to sneak him into the presser?"

"You know him. That's not really his scene."

"What is his scene exactly?"

"European soccer, jazz, cordial liquors, stamp collecting and African artifacts."

"Eh…What did he want, then?"

"Well…"

I could feel her body tense against mine.

"Evidently, my victim was patronizing one of your victims. Number Two, to be exact."

Maddie turned around to face me and scowled. "Arrrggghhh. Great. Just great."

"Yeah. I know."

"How does he know?"

"Say what you want about Jamal, he's got a genuine bloodhound's nose on him."

"And I'm sure he's keeping it under his hat—for now, anyway." She took another sip of wine. Definitely not humming now. "And what does the weasel want?"

"What do you think? He wants a scoop. Just like everybody else in the biz."

"Vultures."

"Well, at least we know—thanks to Jamal—and maybe we can get out in front of this thing."

"Do you think our cases are linked?"

I thought for a moment. Of course, they were linked but only coincidentally—At least that's what I hoped. "Just in a *Strangers on a Train* or ships in the night kind of way. Look, I don't want in on the spotlight. No way. I've had my share. But since when did facts ever matter to a reporter?"

"That's what I'm afraid of. And God forbid they find out about us off-duty. It will be a damned soap opera."

I sighed. She was right. Jamal was right. But it's like getting stuck in the middle of a corn field in a hail storm: There's nothing you can do, really, but stand there and take the beating. Even so, I had to try. "But we can at least stay ahead of the storm."

"Do you think I should tell Sands?"

"Maybe I should talk to him. You know, *unofficial* like. That at least gives him an out for not telling the Captain. He's the one that I'd be worried about."

Maddie nodded. She sipped, then furrowed her brow. "Corporate definitely won't be happy."

"Hey, we're not partners anymore—not on the job—you know what I mean. We don't even work in the same squad."

"But when it comes to facts, Corporate is even worse than journalists. Then, of course, there's city hall."

"Yeah. Rock, meet Hard Place. Hard Place, Rock."

"Damn it." Maddie launched herself off the couch. The wave in her wine crested the glass and sloshed on the floor. "Damn it, Jake."

"Hey. It wasn't me. At least we got a heads up from Jamal before it hit the wire."

"Damn."

I sighed. I nodded.

Complications. I took a gulp of wine and asked myself, *There's always complications, aren't there?*

"Damn it, Jake," Maddie half scolded, half whined, more defeated than angry.

"I know. I know." After a long gap of dead air between us, I asked, "Are you staying?"

"You know I am," Maddie sighed.

Outside, the rumbles of a storm out over the lake bowled their way inland.

~~

The West Bank

With Jamal's information, EC and I worked the late tour, prowling the West Bank. We parked down by the Powerhouse and took the boardwalk along the river north towards the lake. Mid-week, the place was quiet, which somehow made the dark a little bit deeper, a little more ominous. It sucked up sound like a sponge, dulling the occasional traffic noise of a car or truck crossing into or out of the city on the bridges high above.

The West Bank decor was still brick and steel. Lots of old buildings long ago converted from their industrial utility to low rent liquid havens for those looking to escape the daily grind of their working lives, mostly blue collar folks who work with their hands doing the inglorious dirty jobs that society still needs which take a human touch—plumbing, landscaping, putting up new walls or tearing old ones down—or a younger crowd not yet accepting their slavery to a paycheck at jobs they tell themselves are only a stepping stone to something better. Their delusion breeds an angst that seeks out baser pleasures like rainwater following a watershed. The Tiffany tease of the East Bank lights on the ripples of the river only stokes those feelings of class envy. Sometimes into ambition. Sometimes towards something darker.

Hell, it's a paycheck for EC and me.

"I read the interviews on Maddie's case," EC said with a

heavy sigh. "Had to have Q hack the servers downtown. Corporate has things buttoned up pretty tight."

"Yeah. It figures. I'm glad he's on our side."

"He's not on *our* side. He just likes putting it to *The Man.*"

I glanced sideways at EC. "And we're *not* on the same side?"

"I don't want to take sides. I just want to do my job."

"Fair enough." I looked across the river to Dr. Mullaney's high-rise and its tall wall of picture window views of the dark side EC and I prowled. "But good luck with that."

EC grunted.

"At least it's not raining." Nothing worse than doing a foot canvas in the rain. "So what's our play?"

"Swing down to the *Crystal Palace* to talk with the girls, then work our way back up river."

I sighed heavily. Strip clubs were never my cup of tea. You just can't ever scrape all the pheromones off the souls of your shoes. "To the crime scene?"

"It's on the way."

"Hmmm…" We stopped and leaned on the rail to watch an ore boat thrust its way into the river. "Kind of phallic, huh."

EC grunted. The ore boat passed by us so close we could practically touch it. A sailor, silhouetted against the rail by the deck lights, stared down over the side from fifty feet above.

"So, how is Maddie taking all this?" EC asked cautiously.

"About like I am."

"Am I going to need a jumbo-sized bottle of aspirin?"

"Just might. By the time this all shakes out, you just might."

Murder by Munchausen

The ship made the ninety degree turn up the crooked river towards the steel mill. We watched it disappear around the bend, then headed across the parking lot to the *Crystal Palace*.

We flashed our badges to the bouncer and went to the bar to wait for the owner, Fast Eddie, to come out of his office. His nickname wasn't complimentary, having more to do with his staying power than his mental acuity. Fast Eddie is a sprinter, not a marathon man. If desperation has a smell, it is found in the heavy, smoky air of strip clubs—even well-maintained ones like the *Palace* that like to put on an upscale air. Onstage a heavily tattooed blonde worked a meager weekday crowd, mostly foreign sailors who were almost as bored as she was, mechanically going through the motions like a first generation droid. Funny how some vices never leave the human realm. Nobody ties up robots for fun.

"Good evening, gentlemen," Fast Eddie oozed out as he approached us. "Business or pleasure? After all, pleasure is our business."

EC ignored him and held up his phone with a picture of Maddie's second victim on the screen.

"One of the dead ones," Eddie said breezily. "I already talked to a lady cop about her and gave up everything I know—which is nothing really. She didn't work here—on the inside anyway."

"What about this guy?" EC swiped a picture of our victim onto the screen.

Fast Eddie looked at the picture and smiled. "Of course, the judge's son. He's dead, too. Such a shame. There's a lot of that going around these days."

"Good customer?" I asked.

"He hosted a few soirées…mostly for out-of-town business associates, I'm guessing. Though it is our strict policy not to care about whether our receipts find their way onto an IRS form or not."

"On account?" EC asked.

"He was always good for it," Fast Eddie answered with a shrug.

"And dear old dad?" I asked.

"It was a chip I had not yet called in. No need. I run a clean operation…for the most part, anyway. But you know what they say: *'If you're not breaking some law, sometime, you're not drawing breath.'* Damn politicians."

"And the judge's son with the girl?"

"All of our entertainment is on stage—as far as I know and care to. But if a good client wants to bring a magic act in for his private party, who are we to say no?"

"She ever perform her magic tricks for his business associates?"

"Like, *'watch me pull a rabbit out of my hat'* kind of act?" Fast Eddie grinned a toothy smile. "I think she might have done a hat trick or two…or three for the boys. But certainly not here in our establishment."

"And all the party goers were from out of town?"

"Did *you* have to sign in? We don't keep a guest register."

I smiled. "Of course not."

Fast Eddie smiled back. "You understand, then. We uphold the constitutional right to privacy."

"There is no such right," EC muttered.

"Well, I'll have to update our employee handbook, then."

"Do you think there was anything going on between her and the judge's son?" I pressed.

"Not in my job description. That's yours."

"Did the parties stay on this side of the river?"

"There are a few places one can go in the apartment buildings up the hill. But surely you know already that some, ahem, *gentlemen* are known to keep a vacation home there."

"Which one?"

"The Bridge Apartment building, I believe."

"So much for the right to privacy," EC snickered.

"Correct me if I'm wrong, but like doctor-patient confidentiality, I don't believe that right survives death."

"You must have a good lawyer," I noted.

"Did. We *did* have a good lawyer."

I should have known.

The music died and the tattooed blonde marched off the stage.

"Well, thank you for your time, Mr. Duvola," I said.

"Come again, anytime, fellas. Next time, I'll comp you a drink."

EC and I grinned, nodded and then exited the *Crystal Palace* back into the dark, a little more enlightened.

"Always something, ain't it?" EC muttered more to himself than as a legitimate inquiry.

We cut across the parking lot and into a ravine of brick between old warehouse buildings. EC drifted to the opposite sidewalk as we swept the block for any signs of commerce. There were a couple of working girls outside of *McCarthy's*, but their claims of ignorance were confirmed by EC's scan of Maddie's canvas interviews.

We hit the river and crossed the swing bridge to the east side. Upriver a mile or so from the lake, the East Bank quickly shed its ritzy glitter. Seagulls swirled in a cloud behind the ore boat, feasting on the chum whipped, grated and pureed by the ship's prop blade. Their screeching haunted the night air as we approached the alleyway where Ms. Demont met her demise.

EC swept the alley with his flashlight. The crime scene tape was long gone. Rain and industrial grime had washed away or covered the evidence not needed to be collected by Forensics. There were enough casual graffiti doodles to indicate that the alley saw regular foot traffic.

EC sighed. "Not exactly the Poconos."

"No heart-shaped beds, I take it." I surveyed the facades of the neighborhood: a welding shop, a janitorial supplies distributor and, across the street, an empty building available for lease or sale. "Not likely she came all the way here from the *Palace*. Maybe *Mickey's* up the block."

"Yeah. *Mickey's.*" EC said sadly. "That was in the reports. Zero. Zip. Nada."

I looked down the alley. You get a feel that doesn't come through on the crime scene pics. It was a perfect place for delivery on a cheap sexual transaction…or for dispatching a human life. We had been there for ten minutes and not a soul nor a vehicle had passed by. That was plenty of time for the crime—and the gratuitous evisceration.

At the end of the street, a man turned the corner and stopped short at the sight of us by the alley. He turned on his heels and went back the way he came. EC and I swapped a look and followed after him.

At the end of the block, we saw him disappear into *Mickey's*.

"Dumbass shouldn't be wearing a jersey," EC chuckled, as we headed down the block to the bar. "Fifty-seven. Who's that?"

"Can't tell the players without a scorecard." I stopped following professional sports a long time ago.

Murder by Munchausen

We pushed into *Mickey's*. The place was barely open for business. Number 57 was sitting at the far end of the bar staring hard into a pint of lager.

EC and I went down and pulled up stools on either side of the man in the jersey.

He looked right towards EC, then left at me. Then back into the head on his draft.

"You come here often?" I asked, all friendly-like.

He shrugged. "Once in a while."

"After work?" EC asked.

"Yeah. After work. Never before, though."

"So, why did you turn tail and run?"

"Uh, two guys hanging around a dark alleyway where a murder took place? What do you think?"

"Fair enough. Did you know the girl?"

"Cops, right?"

EC showed his shield.

Number 57 sighed heavily. "I'd seen her around."

"Ever make use of her services?"

Jersey guy just shrugged.

"We ain't vice," EC noted.

"Yeah. She discounted on slow nights."

"Red-light specials?"

"Something like that."

"Did you see her the night she died?" EC asked.

"Like I told the other cops—*but hey,* what happened to the lady cop from the TV?"

"We're working a case on the East Bank," I said with just the right amount of disinterest. "Might be related. Might not."

"So, did you see her the night she died?" EC asked again.

"Like I told the other cops, I didn't see anything."

"But you were there, right?"

"I was coming back from the other side to meet some of my buddies. But I didn't see anything."

"Right." I rolled my eyes.

"The file says you saw her and her john duck into the alley," EC asked.

"I was coming back from the *Harbor Inn* and I saw her follow somebody into the alley. I stopped short cause I didn't want to interrupt. The sailors off the boats are usually pretty quick, but they get a bit testy when their shore leave is interrupted. So, I thought I'd wait it out and have a smoke."

"That's it?"

"She was breathing heavy and moaning. Getting all hot and bothered, then suddenly it stopped."

"What stopped?"

"Her breathing heavy. It was, like, totally quiet. Then I heard some sounds. Clinking sounds, like metal on concrete or brick. And some wet sounds. Sloshing like."

"Then what?"

"Then what what?"

"What did you do then?" I enunciated each syllable slowly.

"You read the file. I beat feet back across the river. To heck with my buddies waiting at *Mickey's*. I got pals on the other side, too, you know."

"That's it? You turned tail and ran…*again?*" EC asked, barely masking his disdain.

"I don't need any grief from those foreigners who work the boats. And I don't need any grief from you. I told you the same thing I told the other cops: *I didn't see anything*. I don't know anything and I didn't want to then—*or now.* Are we done?"

EC shook his head in disgust. He looked across at me. "Weasel."

I gave him a nod, but something was gnawing at my gray matter. "Totally quiet?"

"Huh?"

"You said she was breathing heavy and moaning, then it went totally quiet."

"Yeah. You could hear a pin drop."

"What about him?"

"Him who?"

"Sailor boy."

"I didn't see him."

"Did you hear him?"

"Hear him what?"

"Moan or groan or breath heavy or even grunt. It takes two to tango, you know."

As Number 57 thought for a moment, a puzzled look came over his face. "You know, come to think of it, no. I didn't hear him at all."

EC's eyes widened. "Nothing at all?"

"No…Nothing. Nothing at all. He was one quiet dude…whatever he was doing."

"Dude, huh?" I looked at EC and shook my head. "Maybe not so much."

EC squeezed his eyelids shut and massaged the bridge of his nose with his thumb and index finger.

"What do you mean?" Number 57 asked.

"Totally quiet?" I asked again.

"Like church."

"Right. When was the last time you came to Jesus."

"Hey, it's not like you really have to be reminded. Once would be enough to know. My mama took me all the time when I was a kid. Over on Fulton."

"Like church?"

"Like a silent prayer to the baby Jesus himself."

"Damn," was all that EC said.

And I agreed.

EC and I called it a night.

Lt. Sands

After a long walk back to the car and a quiet ride up out of the Flats, EC dropped me off at home. It was four in the morning. I was too wired to sleep and Maddie was at her place, so there was no sense in going to bed—for business or pleasure. After a bird bath in the sink and dragging a brush across my teeth, I went down to the precinct to park myself on the couch in Lt. Sands' office to wait for him to show up. I wanted to get to him first thing. I must have drifted off trying to figure out exactly what to say to him and how to say it, like I promised Maddie I would do.

When I roused myself from a rather lewd dream about Amy at *John's Diner*, my hand was cramped in a death grip on my phone and my nose was filled with the smell of fresh coffee. Lt. Sands was at his desk swiping his way furiously through the overnight arrest reports, like he did every morning. It pays to know what's going on in your own sandbox, even if it's not part of your caseload. Nothing happens in a vacuum—as I was just about to inform the brass. He might be on the bottom rung, but Lt. Sands was still management.

"Morning, sunshine," Lt. Sands said cheerfully followed by a long, loud sip of coffee. He didn't look away from the arrest reports. "Late night?"

"You can't really keep regular hours when you're chasing bad guys. After all, they don't."

"So, did you catch any *bad guys?*"

"Eh…not so much." I sat up.

"You take yours black, right?" Sands pointed at the end table where a cup of coffee steamed to my right.

"Thanks."

"Yeah, well, I had to leave for a moment while you finished your dream about one of my detectives—at least that's what I assumed, but then again you didn't actually call out her name in the throes of your passion."

I sat up and pulled my cup of coffee in front of my face. I breathed in the vapors deeply and sighed them back out again.

"Better exercise your Miranda rights, Jake."

I nodded and sipped.

"I don't mean to appear unhappy to see you…but why were you sleeping in my office?"

"I need to talk to you about Maddie's case."

"Did you talk to her about talking to me?"

"I kind of did."

"Do you really want to get involved?"

"No. But I don't really have a choice."

Lt. Sands finally looked up from the arrest reports at me. I got his attention.

"My vic and one of her vics crossed paths. Number two, to be precise."

"Casually, socially or professionally."

"Professionally, it appears."

He sighed heavily, impatiently. "Out with it."

"Do you want all the gory details? Or just the headlines."

Lt. Sands thought for a moment. "Is it relevant to either case?"

"Could be. Don't know for sure yet. Was there any DNA on number two?"

"There was all kinds of DNA in that alleyway, if I recall. It was a Darwinian cesspool."

"What about on the vic?"

Lt. Sands paused for a beat. "There was…"

"Huh. I'm surprised. Of course, maybe it wasn't the AnSub—I mean, the perp."

"Why is that?"

"Just trying to make sense of a couple of things."

Lt. Sands looked back at his screen and pulled up a report. "We were surprised, too, 'cause it matched out to a dead guy—like a really, really, *really* dead guy. Like a hundred years ago dead."

"What the—"

"Exactly. Collected in an unsolved case back in prehistoric times when the technology was new."

"Where? Here?"

Sands scrolled down. "Nah. Boston. A murder case, too—how's that for a coincidence?"

I shrugged, but in my mind I was paging through my stack of books back at the apartment.

"The original allele panel was pretty fractured, but tech went with the theory that it might actually be a residual transfer of familial material, but the genealogy trace dead ended in the last millennium. It was probably just a bad sample collection in the original case."

"Yeah. Okay. That's probably it." Though I really didn't believe it. Inside the box thinking.

"So, about the connection with your case." Sands folded

his hands in front of me and looked me dead in the eye. He was a good cop and knew there was something more.

There was, but I hadn't even told Maddie yet. I met his stare and held it.

"Jake…?"

I shook my head slightly.

"Right." He looked away to straighten items on his desktop.

"I just wanted to give you a heads up on the vics. I'm not crashing Maddie's case, but it's out there."

"In the press?"

I nodded.

"Great."

"Just one guy has it and it's under wraps for now, but I can't keep a lid on it forever. I got promises to keep."

"Do I want to know?"

I thought for a moment and shook my head. "Honestly? Probably not. Not yet."

"Great."

"You tell me how you want to handle this and I'll do it."

Lt. Sands just nodded. "Let me think about it."

I got up to go.

"And maybe you can check your wet dreams at the door next time."

I felt my face flush, so I chopped out a quick Boy Scout salute, then left.

~~~

Exit Alley

I walked down the alley—"Exit Alley" as it was known in the House. The regular precinct guys called it that because it leads to the "Geek Squad" offices, which they viewed as a revolving door out of a career in public service for any "real" cop. Maybe it was, but that would be a slow turning door for me. I wasn't going anywhere fast or soon—personally or professionally. I've got nothing else better to do. So in my mind, I went all Sartre on the situation during idle moments of the day—like just then as I waited for EC to show up for our tour—pondering its ramifications as "Existential Alley," a contested frontier borderline between humanity with all its messy mental and emotional implications and the creepy shadow world of…Robantiy? Binarykind? Digi Sapiens? A cold, bloodless and soulless man-made species untouched by the finger of God walking upright amongst us.

Robots were great when they were securely locked behind their safety cages in automated factories, picking and placing, welding and painting, doing all the mindlessly repetitive and hazardous labors that previously led to injury, death, labor unions and civil lawsuits. Nobody gets sued when a machine wears out its bearings. Nobody strikes when new technology threatens the job description of last generation AI. No unemployment benefits are paid out when a one-trick robot is no longer needed to satisfy the material needs of fickle human beings in a free market economy.

Everybody sneers at what I do: solving crimes they've convinced themselves aren't real crimes, because they're not real living, breathing perps. But the vics are real enough. Oh, sure, the judge's son's homicide made lead story headlines, but that was because of the victim and who he was—or more correctly who his father was—not because of any human interest in the perpetrator. Robotic criminals have no personalities. No Jack the Ripper. No Charlie Manson. No Ted Bundy. Just a cold, hard machine, with means but no motive; no behavioral profiles; no evil smiles; no dark empathetic links to the hidden urges in our own psyches that draws us to them with an unseen force like metal to a magnet. Nobody goes out to get a beer with the paint robot in a car factory. The public doesn't hungrily follow news feeds about malfunctioning machines, like they do Maddie's case. *No simpatico.* No 'there but for the grace of God go I,' as victim…*or killer.*

But I knew. The hundred-year-old DNA in Maddie's case was a real clue. So was the statement of Number 57 from *Mickey's* about hearing the physiological grunts, moans and heavy breathing of Maddie's victim but not her perp. And, especially, the stylized staging of internal organs that hearkened back to the very first serial murderer ever in London during the late 1800s and an unsolved copycat spree a hundred years ago in New England. I'll bet the *"real"* police up at the other end of *Exit Alley* didn't even look into that hundred-year-old case file.

Murder by Munchausen stories in the press were regarded like messy car accidents: the fleeting horror of mangled metal and flesh, not the cold shadow of evil showing its ugly face that great narratives are made of. Maybe not so much anymore.

I knew things were about to change. It would make Jamal happy…and wealthy.

I pondered my aimless doodles of arrows, cubes and fighter planes on the pad of paper. Just then EC waltzed in. I knew he would not be happy about my theory—but inconvenienced unhappy, not mad unhappy like Maddie and the brass will be.

EC saw my face and abruptly stopped at my desk.

"Jake?"

I shook my head and sighed.

"Crap."

~~~

No Anchovies

EC and I sat at Cutty's waiting for our "pizza with no anchovies" to be delivered. Even though it was nine in the morning, the lingering dredges of the night tour made the place almost half full. It was about the quietest time of the day for the deli—just what we needed for our meet.

It doesn't matter how dressed down a Fed gets for casual Friday, they still reek of arrogance, like PGA Tour pros smacking balls at a local hacker's driving range. He marched up to our table, his back ram-rod straight, and peered down at us with a look of disdain that had been long ago practiced into the standard DC default resting bitch face.

"Men."

EC and I looked up at the *federale* towering over us.

"Have a seat," I offered.

EC just stared up at the Secret Service man dripping with superciliousness for us, for Cutty, and for citizenry at large.

"No time. No need." He dropped a thick envelope onto the table between EC and me.

"Actually, I'm surprised to see you here—out here in *public.*"

"Yeah, well, you start asking the wrong questions, you draw attention to yourself, the wrong kind of attention."

"Our spook friends?"

He nodded. "I was warned. Now you are, too."

"Another black mark on my permanent record."

"You owe me."

"For what? The black mark?" I tapped the envelope. "Or this?"

"For the warning." He turned to leave.

"Hey, what about your *quid pro quo?*"

"I'll take an I.O.U. on that, Jake. I wouldn't touch anything you've got right now with a level A hazmat suit. I have a pension to consider."

We watched the door ooze shut behind the Secret Service agent. The ego level of the deli retreated from the red line on the dial.

EC looked at the envelope, then up at me. "Great. Now, we've got the Feds mad at us."

"They are always mad at someone. It might as well be us."

I reached for the envelope, but EC grabbed my hand. "Not here."

"Where?"

"Your place?"

I nodded.

"What are you doing bringing his kind in here?" Cutty stood over us and barked out his question. "I run a respectable establishment."

"Sorry, Cutty," EC said in sing-song fashion, like a four-year-old busted by his dad for stealing cookies.

Cutty growled. "I hate those guys. They tip lousy and generally piss off the staff with their demands."

"How did you ever know?"

"Well, for starters, do they have those Ray-Bans surgically implanted or did he inherit his momma's eyes?"

Murder by Munchausen

"So, Cutty, can we get a couple of pastrami Reuben's to go with no anchovies?"

"Anchovies? There ain't no anchovies on a Reuben."

"Exactly."

We got our sandwiches and left.

~~~

Federal Code

Back at my place, we tore into the envelope. Lots of pages with lots of words and lots of trademark Federale black magic marker redaction. Reading it was like a ride in an antique manual clutch-type car driven by a novice—jerky stop-and-go. I let EC plow through it and went to get the stack of books piled away in the corner.

I sorted through the first few, discarding them to the side, until I came to a yearbook-looking tome of Twentieth Century crimes. I turned to the page I had already bookmarked about a serial killer case from the late Twentieth Century in Boston. Unsolved, all the victims were working girls who were strangled then gutted in back alleys down by the bay. There were only five, so the case never caught on nationally—not at a time when Bundy and the Green River killer were running rampant. Besides, the killings stopped abruptly, so without any fresh blood the news media flamed out and quickly lost interest in a story going nowhere. I guess not much has changed. There was some initial rumble about it being a copycat crime for Jack the Ripper, but that didn't seem to get much traction with John Q. Public outside of Boston. Beantown was hyped up about it for a few months, but pretty soon the lack of empathetic victims, a single-digit body count, and a perp that suddenly went Rip Van Winkle, just like the original, wasn't shiny enough to distract people from their daily lives.

The thing was, though, that the killer's signature wasn't just a ripoff of old Jack from 1880s London. He went one better and looped the intestines around the victim's neck and made it look like a half-Windsor knot—*just like Maddie's vics,* who were also all working girls, who were also killed down by a waterfront—just not in Boston. Great. A copycat of a copycat. I read through the case, looking to see if there was any DNA evidence. Back then, the science was there, but there was a pretty limited database to match against, so it ended up being merely confirming or exclusionary evidence. The detectives back then actually had to detect. There was DNA. Unmatched, therefore unsolved.

"Great," I blurted out to myself.

"What's that?" EC looked up from the government file.

"Looks like Maddie's case has some strings attached—back a couple of centuries or so."

"Huh? What does that have to do with our case? Sure, our guy may have patronized her establishment, but he was dead when she hit the pavement. And that's her headache. There ain't enough aspirin in a Drug Mart to get me to want to share that pain."

"Yeah, but I got a gut feel it's a Geek Squad deal."

"Come on, Jake. She's got a perp with a blood thirst. Androids don't got blood, so they don't get a thirst for it. They're just machines."

"Yeah, but they are machines programmed by warm-blooded creatures."

"What are you saying?"

"You saw her crime scene and her vics?"

EC nodded. "So?"

I spun the book around and slid it towards EC's end of the couch.

He looked at the pics and nodded, then turned the pages. "Crap."

"Sands told me they have DNA—DNA that doesn't ping anyone still drawing breath or ever has since it started becoming part of birth records."

"How can that be?"

"Right. How can that be."

"But it gets a forensics hit off the old CODIS system?"

"To an unsolved case in Boston." I tapped my index finger on the crime scene photos in the open book between us. "But that guy's been six feet under for a long, long time."

"Exactly, so why would that DNA show up now and show up here...*and how?*"

I shrugged my shoulders.

"Man, nobody's gonna want to hear this."

"Think about what the guy at Mickey's said about what went down in the alley that night. What if somebody—maybe some medical spook type—reverse engineered biological material off the alleles from CODIS to plant at a crime scene? Alleles that match a crime from, say, Boston, from, say, the last century?"

"And then programmed a droid to re-enact the crime."

I nodded. "And where does our victim's wife work?"

"The Clinic."

"In Genetics."

"Damn." EC shook his head wearily. "Got any aspirin?"

"I don't believe in headaches. Like luck and leprechauns." I got up and headed to the kitchen. "But I've got beer."

"That'll do."

I came back with a couple of cold ones and handed a long neck to EC. "So, what did my friend at the Secret Service dig up for us?"

"I think we're going to have to have Q take a look, but from what I can tell, it looks like the code was used to ghost the AnSub on the Atlas Grid by tapping into it and swapping out metadata. Not exactly something that's easily done—spook level stuff for sure. Only someone with an NSA tie-in or back door could pull it off. But that way, the droid could move undetected throughout the city—or the country for that matter, a Class B felony for starters. You just can't have machines out there unidentified and untracked, but this guy did it."

"I wonder if Maddie even thought to pull the Atlas metadata for the Flats."

"Why would she?"

"Yeah. Why. Nobody's thinking Munchhausen for her crimes." I took a long pull of Shiner Bock. "But maybe they should."

"I don't want any part of it."

"Me neither, partner. Me neither, too."

"But we don't really have a choice, do we?"

I shook my head. "Let's go roust Q."

~~~

Mad Scientists

Back at Exit Alley, Q poured over the stack of papers from the Feds. He looked up and shook his head. "Damn it, I really wish we had gotten the original digital files on these, 'cause the back channel data would be a tapioca treat for sure. But, if they came from where I think they did…"

"Spook Central?" I queried.

Q just looked at me, speechless for once, without a smart-aleck come back. His face was dead serious, a look not often seen.

"So, this isn't going to help?" EC asked impatiently.

"I didn't say that." Q cracked a mad scientist grin. "I'm just going to have to get creative."

"How's that?"

"Why don't you just leave that to me. It's like Chinese takeout: you might not want to see the kitchen if you want to enjoy the meal."

"Like if you're a cat lover?" I asked.

"Tastes just like chicken," Q smirked. "What I can tell you right now is that this is a very clever fellow. He's found a way to create digital shadows in Atlas and move through them. That's not a huge deal. It can be done, eh, easy enough for a mad genius like me, but usually, it causes disturbances in the metadata that can be observed, like little digital ripples in the Grid's space-time continuum. You can't see the fish, but you can see him move beneath the water—if you know where to look and what to look for. The beauty of this fellow's hack is not the shadows but the backfill. He's not only figured out a way to move without being seen but to digitally brush the sand back over the footprints of his mechanical minion."

"So, not your typical chop-shopper."

"I should say not."

EC pinched his eyes shut and massaged the bridge of his nose.

"From the pizza our delivery boy gave us, do you think the spooks are on to him?"

Q scoffed out loud. "Come on, Jake, you're talking about guys that fish with hand grenades. This is eloquent and subtle…*and beautiful.*"

I looked at EC, who shook his head in mild disbelief at Q's reverie of rapture over machine code.

"But not *too* subtle for you, right?"

Q smiled his mad scientist grin. "This craftsmanship is definitely not bureaucratically inspired. It's art—it's not only art, it's Picasso. A game changer."

"Can you find him?"

"Honestly? I don't know. This is *primo,* major league stuff."

"So what do we do?"

"Do you know how gulls and terns fish? They loiter on high and scan the surface, waiting for a flash of light, a reflection of the sun off the shiny scales of their prey."

"And how are you going to do that without help from the Feds."

Q rolled his eyes. "I don't need their help. The grid is like Swiss cheese—full of holes."

"So what then?" asked EC curtly. Even he was losing patience.

"I need to do my trolling without them seeing and knowing."

"Good luck with that, then."

"Huh." Q was suddenly distracted.

"What is it?"

"Well, it seems like such a…I don't know, such an incongruity. This is truly Mensa mad scientist quality stuff."

"Yeah? So?"

"To kill a spouse in a bitter divorce? You don't hire Michelangelo to whitewash a fence."

"The Pope did."

"Yeah, well, in our day and age, that's what they make droids for."

"What? To kill spouses? Or to paint?"

"To paint. But killing spouses is chop shop level stuff. Not museum quality art."

"Well, you did say that he's a *mad* scientist."

"I did. Quite mad. Mad like me. After all, I'm a scientist, too."

"Takes one to catch one?"

"Give me a few days to dig into this."

"And while you're at it…" I wrote down the dates and times of Maddie's murders and passed the scrap of paper to Q. "No footprints or breadcrumbs on this."

"Your case?"

I shook my head. "You don't want to know. Corporate is all over this, so don't even look for it. Just see if you see any flashes in the grid."

"Maddie's—"

"Don't ask. Don't think about it. Just let me know."

Q nodded, read the dates, then got up and fed the paper into a shredder. "That's the beauty of the old analog ways—you can actually destroy things and make them go away for good."

"Yeah. Kind of like murder."

"Yeah. Kind of."

~~~

Infinite Will

Machines might have infinite will and patience but zero passion. Without any will to break nor passion to succeed, I never found synthoid sports of much interest. No glory in victory or grace in defeat, just battle bot mayhem. The sports world had devolved into sterile weekly contests of grinding gears and Herculean hydraulic strength, devoid of any creativity and lacking in the pleasures of the unsuspected and unexpected. After all, the "coaches" were just programmers relying on statistical analysis for their play calling, so the games and competition had become merely mechanical logic contests played out in modern day coliseums. No doubt that is why the leagues reached back into their hall of fames to resurrect personalities to graft onto their atheledroids, but, even still, sports is about as engaging as computer models of the weather. At least for me.

Maddie's case made me realize that, like synthoid sports, I had been just going through the motions in the Geek Squad. Android crime was more puzzle than pursuit of perps, *real* perps. Maybe the cops up the alley were right. Maybe that was really why Maddie's case piqued my interest.

Sure, we had our victims and all, but even a petty criminal has some passion driving him to try to rob a C-store or break into someone's suburban castle—even if it is a pharmaceutically induced passion. They are still driven creatures, not logic executing machines that look eerily human-like. Solving the crimes that found their way down Exit Alley to me and EC was mostly mechanical and formulaic. The machines had their grid logs and they had their flash memories that Q and the boys pulled and decoded for us. Then, the hunt was on to go out to find them and pick them up like a repo man, not a detective. Even the murders by Munchausen. Most times…

Something was definitely different now. I didn't so much know it as I sensed it. I couldn't sort it out at my desk in the sterile cubicles of Exit Alley, so I bolted to wander the streets and let my feet do my thinking. I eventually ended up in Public Square in time to sit like a rock in the rapids of rush hour as the city drained of its drones…*and droids.*

I sat and picked the synthoids out of the crowd like spotting four-leaf clovers in an unkempt lawn. They are there, but most people can never find them. I let the ones that are different catch my eye. Same with droids. You can't really search for them. You have to *let* yourself see them. Unlike four-leaf clovers, though, there are far, far more of them in the crowd. Suddenly, I felt the oppressive invasion of our lives by machines. Of course, technology was everywhere scraping away always on our humanity, making us more and more dependent on it, addicted to it really. I imagine the empty vacuum of all your data going dark is like the junkie's crash as he comes down off his high. We have to have our data fix, just like he's got to have his chemicals.

The industry has its statistics about market penetration for their PSAs. They also have their "heartwarming" anecdotes of all that they do for mankind, for the sick, the needy and, especially, the children. All the dirty work. All the dangerous work. All the jobs that were once done by the poor souls in some dark corner of the world colonized and enslaved—physically in the ancient times, economically and culturally over the last century—whose lives were infinitely more wretched than the "civilized" folks who exploited them for their own comforts. I briefly wondered whatever happened to those less fortunate citizens of the world, but then I went back to visually picking digital fleas out of the rush hour crowd. Even though humans still far outnumbered synthoids, they seemed a malevolent presence, like cancer cells waiting, perhaps multiplying with the bad habits of their host.

But now, instead of just mindless agents of harm driven by hacker code at the behest of a calculating spouse, I sensed the manifestation of a passion to do evil. In the cases that Maddie and I were working a glint of that passion, of that evil beneath the surface, caught my eye—like Q described about the way gulls and terns fish. I had seen the flash in our crimes and now looked in vain for it again in the legions of machines that moved among us.

The hacker or bureaucrat or spook who was pulling the strings on these droids that killed a judge's son and the sex workers on the West Bank was doing more than providing a service, more than just automating murder. He was chasing his own internal demons through these machines. I wondered if there was true satisfaction by proxy. There would have to be. Droids malfunction and droids can be programmed to execute a crime, but to become a serial killer, there has to be a driving human passion that comes from somewhere deep and dark within a disturbed human psyche.

I waited for Maddie to meet me and witnessed the infection of society, wondering if the good doctor who had her husband killed knew who she was working with…or was wrestling with her own demons.

~~~

Love is a Battlefield

Maddie came at me out of the sun like an ancient Japanese Zero pilot from some World War a long, long time ago. "So…you come here often, sailor?"

She knew I did. We spent a lot of time together sitting on the bench by the Soldiers and Sailors monument, observing the foot traffic in Public Square when we were partners on the job. Sometimes to decompress. Sometimes to talk out a case. Most times just to people watch and have a few chuckles at humanity's expense. I still came quite a bit, though mostly alone anymore. I shaded my eyes and tried to look up into her face. It had been a while—a week, maybe? Or more, since we connected. It happened, though usually for a day or two, when we both got caught up in cases that were intensifying towards an arrest.

"I got your favorite." She held out a bag of warm cashews and a red delicious apple like we used to get inside the Rapid Transit station. "Angelo says 'hey' by the way."

"Thanks." I took a bite of apple and tossed back a couple nuts. "Pull up a bench."

She sat down beside me. "Boy, it's been a while since we hung out here. What's up?"

I munched and thought. Everything is a negotiation with Maddie, a mini-battle. She was definitely feisty and always testing boundaries. Not like Amy at *John's Diner*. That was simple. Maddie always took forethought and planning and maneuvering.

"How's your case going?"

Maddie sighed heavily. She stroked the top of my thigh as she scanned the crowd in the Square. "Kind of all consuming…but I guess I'm not telling you anything you don't already know. Sorry, Jake."

"Comes with the turf."

Maddie nodded and sighed. "How's yours?"

"Looking seriously at the wife. Gonna follow up at the Clinic campus tomorrow."

"What I wouldn't give to have an angle to chase. We're buried in leads from John Q. Public."

"Yeah, the press will do that for you. Any of them any good?"

"Not yet. At least Sands has thrown out some overtime for patrol guys to help on the phones. Still…"

"He told me about the DNA."

"Yeah, a dead end."

"Yeah…or maybe not." I offered Maddie some cashews, but she declined, like a pitcher shaking off a catcher's signal.

"What are you talking about? There's no database match."

"Did you check the case file for that DNA?"

"It was a murder in Boston—from ages ago. Unsolved."

"Did you check out the crime scene photos?"

Maddie shook her head. "They weren't online. Never scanned in, probably, but I browsed the murder book."

"Curious about the DNA match."

"It's not a great sample. They didn't get a complete panel,

so it wasn't really a true match. You know how the science was back then."

I looked at Maddie. "You know it's a copycat, right?"

She held my stare, then looked away. "I doubt it, Jake. Too obscure. Just your ADHD imagination working overtime."

We watched a wave of pedestrians flood the crosswalk, then drain until the last drip of humanity hit the curb as the light went green and traffic started into the intersection.

I took a loud bite of apple. She was too good an investigator to believe what she had just said.

Maddie swiveled her head back and forth taking a last quick look at the Square, then patted my thigh. "I gotta get back. I'd love to stay and just hang out. Really, I would, but…"

"But duty calls."

"Maybe this weekend?" She grabbed my hand and took a bite of apple.

"You bet."

She smiled and planted a wet sticky kiss on my forehead, then left.

I watched her go and wondered if Q had gotten a glimpse of our Munchhacker as he moved through the clouds.

I didn't want Maddie's case, but it was coming at me. She'd see that too, eventually—if she didn't already.

I ignored EC's texts and calls. Once the rush hour finished draining the city, I went back home alone for the night.

~~~

The Clinic

EC moped the whole way over to the East side where the Clinic campus sprawled out over fifty city blocks with towering monuments to Neurology, Cardiology, Ophthalmology, Cancer and the good doctor's specialty, Genetics.

Only when the cruiser pulled into the parking lot did he say anything. "So, what gives?"

"I know. I know. I should have answered, but I…but I tried to talk to Maddie yesterday."

"No go?"

"She ain't buying it—at least not consciously. I think some small suspicion might be gnawing at the back of her mind, though."

EC sighed heavily. "I don't want any part of her serial killer party."

"Hmmm…" I kept my thoughts to myself.

"So, what do you hope to find here?"

"Well, there's no money trail. And *Doctor* Mullaney doesn't seem to have much of a social life at all, so there's got to be something going on at work. Not to mention the hundred-year-old DNA in Maddie's case."

EC grunted. "Well, Q's hack into her patient files came up empty handed."

"So, we see what we see. Good old fashion police work."

"I hate stakeouts."

"Come on, man, it's why we make the big bucks."

"And I hate hospitals."

I just nodded, remembering the vigil over Patty's last hours. I raised my fist. "On three?"

EC mirrored me. On three, my paper covered his rock, so I got to wander the halls while he parked himself in a far corner of the huge waiting area outside our person of interest's office. I got back to spell him at eleven.

"Got to get some serious air," my partner said over his shoulder as he beat feet for the nearest exit.

I settled in for my shift of watching paint dry. Genetics is definitely white collar health care. No bloody lab coats or body parts being hauled away in plastic bags emblazed with the old Dow Chemical biohazard symbol. Dr. Mullaney was actually something of a modern day witch doctor who brewed up genetically modified *flora* and *fauna* extracts based on patient genome modeling to treat infectious diseases and molecular disorders. It was all voodoo to me, but her intimacy with DNA gave me pause.

Unlike the ER, the foot traffic in and out of her office was leisurely, mostly patients with the occasional lab-coated colleague, scrub-suited nurse, polo-shirted administrative type or latex-gloved housekeepers with their cleaning carts coming and going—much more quickly than the time required for a consultation. Synthoids passed by, but never entered her suite of exam rooms. I passed the time browsing online for dead trees stained with ink and watching the ebb and flow of her clients in search of a cure.

At eleven-thirty sharp, Dr. Mullaney emerged from her office and headed towards the cafeteria. I blended into a clot of patients and loved ones headed in that general direction and followed her. Finally, a change of scenery.

Her heels clicked on the tile floor of the corridor with the hypnotic regularity of a metronome. My mind drifted and I didn't take notice of the man in the jumpsuit pushing a maintenance cart towards us until the *ritardando* in Dr. Mullaney's pace closed the gap between us and I thought she might notice me. Instead, their eyes met and locked, pulling their heads towards each other as they passed until she shook her head ever so slightly and picked her pace back up to *andantino*.

Pretending to consult a building directory, I watched the man follow Dr. Mullaney's retreat over his shoulder. When he looked back, I read disappointment and frustration scrawled in his furrowed brow. My spidey sense tingled.

I quickly texted EC to hand off the tail of Dr. Mullaney and waited for the maintenance man and his cart to pass by. The patch on his jumpsuit declared his name to be Jeffrey. I inventoried him quickly: Caucasian; late twenties or early thirties; approximately six foot tall; lean, maybe a hundred eighty pounds—*maybe;* sandy hair; dark eyes. It was the eyes. They were not only dark in color but harbored a human darkness behind them.

Reeling Jeffrey out enough to be discreet, I followed his long and winding path through the maze of Clinic corridors. Just as doubt began to percolate in my mind, he parked his cart next to a synthoid that had broken down outside the Radiology Department and was twitching like it had Tourette's Syndrome.

As I passed by, Jeffrey tapped the droid's diagnostic port and stared at the screen of his *iSlate*.

~~~

The Baron

The alley cam was off. Q, EC and I huddled close to the door to keep from getting rained on. Even though we were outside the building, the discussion unfolded in hushed tones.

"M.I.T.?" Q asked.

"Full ride," EC answered. "Never finished, though."

"I knew *the Baron* was top shelf in the gray matter department. Gotta be to worm-hole the NSA servers."

"Jeffery also had some issues with anger and small animals in his youth. He never really did play well with others."

"And you're sure this is the guy?"

"Yeah, he really hits the sweet spot on a BAU profile," I added.

EC scowled, then asked Q, "You think you can do it?"

"I can. But 'should I' is the question." Q's eyes darted my way without turning his head. "You got paperwork on this?"

EC groaned a little under his breath.

"Ah, so suddenly you're a bureaucratic purist?" I teased.

Q turned and sneered in my direction. "Only when it's *my* ass on the line."

"Come on, man. You do this kind of stuff all the time for shits and giggles."

"Corporations are paranoid patsies. Trolling their waters is like cruising PTA meetings for MILFs. If you get lucky, nobody's going to say anything afterwards for the sake of the kids."

"Kids?" EC wondered.

"Customers—whatever." Q sighed. "This is different. They play for keeps. I kind of like having my life…unperturbed by big brother's intrusions."

"Look, we're not asking you to go out and attack the ramparts—"

"What's a rampart?"

I rolled my eyes. "Don't be a wuss."

"Hey, I'm the one playing tunnel rat and going in after him. Not you."

"We're not asking you to steal state secrets," EC blurted out in frustration. "Just follow his footprints."

"Yeah, into the creepy spook house at the end of the street. It's one thing to play peeping Tom and look into the place over the fence or through a window. Another thing altogether to go in the front door, wander around and come out the back way."

"Well, how is he doing it?" I narrowed my eyes at Q. *"Mister Super Genius…"*

"This guy is pushing code through the Atlas grid structure to commit murder—"

"So you say," Q cut EC off.

"No. So *you* say. That's what you told us," EC snapped impatiently back at Q. "This guy has figured out a way to drop and pull command libraries into droids to commit crimes. That data traffic has to move on the grid, in and out of the cloud, right?"

Q finally, reluctantly nodded. "I told you he's ghosting the grid and not leaving any breadcrumbs. I didn't know he's worm-holing through the NSA servers in Utah."

"You've seen the Baron going in, but you can't trace when or where or how he comes back out. We just want to know when and where that code is hitting the grid on the download."

Q blew a long, wispy exhale. "But you know where this is going to lead. Corporate is going to come down on us like a ton of bricks, especially if we lay a big stink bomb on their high profile case."

We all looked down the alley at the precinct house.

"But we might just save a life," I said softly.

"Damn." Q beat his fist against the wall. "You always go all Superman righteous and moral on me."

EC Smiled.

Q turned on his heels and pulled open the door. "I'll set up the bloodhound code. But I *have* to put a self-destruct into my algorithms, just in case the NSA starts knocking on our—on *my* door. So, I'm not making any guarantees."

"How soon?" I asked.

"It'll be up tonight." As Q went inside, he called over his shoulder. "Good luck."

"Yeah. Right." I looked at EC. "If it wasn't for bad luck…"

"I wouldn't have no luck at all…"

The security camera light came back on.

And so we waited.

~~~

Waiting Games

Waiting is always the worst part. Waiting for Mechanical. Waiting for Q. Waiting for the Baron to come out of his wormhole again.

I passed the time nursing a plate of ravioli and a half carafe of Chianti at *Maria's*.

"Hey, sailor…buy me a drink?" Jamal flopped himself down across from me in the back booth that over the years had come to have my name on it.

I grunted. *Why does everybody call me 'sailor?'*

He took out his phone and snapped a pic of me shoveling down a ravioli. "I hear this place serves great paparazzi."

"For your editor?"

"He insists. Otherwise, my expense report gets kicked back—unpaid, of course." Jamal filled the wine glass at his place setting from my carafe. He took a sip and scowled. "House wine."

"Snob."

"Yeah, but you're paying and I'm not proud."

When Maria's daughter, Gina, came by our table, Jamal ordered a plate of *Carbonara*. I nodded when she drained the last bit of Chianti into my glass and held up the empty carafe.

"Why is it you always show up around meal time?"

"Do I?" Jamal asked, acting innocent.

"Like a buzzard on road kill."

"Hey, I pride myself on being a professional. So, *detective,* how goes the war on crime?"

"You know. Hurry up and wait. Our Clinic guy moonlights at the VA and EC is connecting the dots between hardware serial numbers from their spares inventory and our droid perp. Thank God I've got a partner who likes doing puzzles."

"So, Maddie's gonna cross the finish line first, then, eh?"

"What do you mean?"

Jamal sat back with a silly smile on his face as Gina delivered his dinner. "You really should make more of an effort to stay informed on current events."

I watched the reporter dig into his pasta.

"In fact, I'm just fueling up on my way to the big press conference to announce an arrest."

"You know it's bull crap."

"Now, now. No sour grapes, Jakie."

"You don't arrest synthoids. And I'm here to tell you this one just won't stick on a human."

"Your DNA copycat theory?"

I nodded.

"I like your story better, but they must have something good to assemble the media."

"Don't buy it, man."

Jamal just smiled around a mouthful of garlic bread. "I never do. Just like dinner. Hey, you don't mind if I take a copy of the receipt, do you?"

"Double dipping?"

"It helps pay the bills."

"In our business, it's called fraud."

"Come on, Jake, neither of us wants the IRS looking over our shoulder."

I shrugged.

Jamal slurped up the last piece of fettuccine off his plate and wiped the sauce from his chin. "Gotta bolt. Don't want to be late for the *really* big news."

"Don't buy it."

"Hey, you know me. Just keep me in the loop on the truth."

Gina came up to the booth. "One check or two?"

I looked at Jamal. "Put it on my tab."

"You're a prince, Jake." Jamal grinned and diner-dashed to the front door before I could change my mind.

I finished my wine, stewing in the news about Maddie's case. Then, I wandered back to the building and fired up my *iSlate*.

Maddie got her pretty face plastered all over the local news feeds. Watching the stream of the press conference, I hadn't seen so much brass in one place since the last time I was at the range. The Commissioner stood at the podium claiming victory over evil with the precinct Captain so close his bad breath might have been fogging the Commissioner's cuff links. Maddie hung back with her partner, Lieutenant Sands and the rest of the task force at the back of the dais.

While the Commissioner prattled on about the greatness of *his* department, I scanned the arrest reports. Responding to a call to roust the city's dreck from the posh East Bank and herd them back to the other side of the river, a patrol unit found a bloody knife in possession of one of the homeless interlopers. Well, maybe possession is a bit of a stretch. Let's just say they both occupied the same pile of trash out back of *Sammy's* restaurant. The blade was the right size and shape to have been handy in eviscerating a corpse—or carving medallions of beef tenderloin. The homeless man was correctly aged and Caucasian to fit the F.B.I. Behavior Analysis Unit profile, with the requisite history of mental issues and a sketchy track record of taking his prescribed medications. As for an alibi, well, he didn't really seem to know where he was in the present moment, let alone weeks and months ago at the time of the crimes.

Once the Commissioner and the Captain were done boasting about their leadership, Maddie stepped forward to take questions. The camera definitely loves her. Most of the questions were pretty routine and she handled them with ease, though the attractive info babe from *Action News 5* got a scratch from Maddie's claws when she asked a particularly stupid question about lab results. Of course, the blood work wouldn't be back from the lab yet.

I was about to click off when Jamal stood to ask whether the suspect had any medical training in his background. Her hesitation in answering was so slight that unless you knew Maddie and could read her expressions like I could, the assembled reporters all missed that the question had snagged on a lingering doubt in her mind.

"We are still working to assure ourselves that all the blanks on Mr. Steinmauer are filled in accurately," she stonewalled.

Before she could move on, Jamal called out, "And is all of the DNA accounted for?"

"Oh, man..." I moaned out loud. The old Boston DNA information had never been released by the police. I swore that

Murder by Munchausen

Maddie's glare bored right through the cameras directly into my chest.

"As I told Channel Five, we are still waiting on lab results," she replied curtly.

After the exchange, I clicked off. Even if the blood on the knife came back as a match to any one of Maddie's victims, that wouldn't close the deal for me. My gut feeling on seeing their guy's mug shot was that this perp wouldn't make the grade for the murders. There was confusion in his eyes, not evil.

Out back on the fire escape, I turned a lawn chair towards the west and parked myself in it with my feet up on the hand rails to watch the sunset, hoping Q's bloodhound code would pick up the Baron's scent.

Between sips of Cabernet, I pondered how the ancient Greek mythological aether eventually turned out to be real: the invisible radio waves that filled the space between me and the horizon were literally the breaths of the government gods that lorded over all of us. We were all tethered to the Atlas grid with our *iNodes* or *Alpha-Bits,* trading the immediate gratification of human whims for the unseen manipulation of our Gamma waves by the malicious winds that blow only that information and those options across the face of our gaze that some AI algorithm has determined for the sake of society or commerce is best for the greater good. We're just digital fish swimming in a sea of data, not realizing how wet we are.

I ignored an incoming call from Maddie. Even though the presser had ended, her tour was far from over. There was paperwork to be done, no doubt, and I didn't want to take away her adrenalin high. On a more selfish note, not being up for an emotional scrum at the moment, I didn't want to face her wrath for sharing confidential info with Jamal.

Out there in the aether, everything human floated above and around us like a binary shadow of our world. Moving through it all the time was the natural evil of men, though typically it was merely a reflection of corporeal. A few used that shadow world to move their ill intents out and beyond themselves.

The sun went down. I refilled my glass, waiting for the ping that meant Q's digital hunt had flushed our quarry.

~~~

Perchance to Dream

I nodded off and slept fitfully on the couch, alternating between a recurring dream of Amy—the same one I had in Lt. Sands' office—and a new nightmare I'd never had before. Some people's dreams are surreal like a classic Tim Burton movie, but mine are usually hyper-realistic, almost flashbacks, especially when they're work related. So much so I'd kid Maddie there should be overtime on my pay stub for them.

I should have been reliving the warehouse takedown of the bodega AnSub with EC, but I didn't know where I was and my partner was nowhere to be found. Outside, I prowled down an empty city street through the cones of light thrown down by street lamps, in and out of blinding light followed by a hood of total darkness. I couldn't tell if I was headed somewhere or just going in circles. The storefronts were dark and unmarked. Animal sounds like out of a jungle bounced off the brick and concrete, hauntingly human at times, but only compounding my disorientation. Gripping so hard on my Glock the checkering dug painfully into my palms. No glass. No comm. No partner. No backup. No choice but to keep moving forward, but not knowing why. Sweating, but not hot. Gulping air, but not winded. Every muscle taut, then wound tighter yet as a door to my right creaked open, spilling a dim light into my path. Back to the entryway wall, I followed my Glock through the doorway and slid right into my recurring dream of Amy. She lay naked on my bed, but was melting into a pool of red on the floor like a Salvador Dali clock, flowing lazily toward a rear door that I could see led back to the street I had just left—

Until the *iCore* notification from Q hit my phone in 911 mode.

As I came back up to break the surface of reality, grabbing at the air with my lungs, my mind's eye glimpsed a blurry silhouette disappearing into the darkness between the street lights.

I peered squintily at the screen for Q's message, but it was blank except for the record of his call and the time: two-forty in the morning. As I scratched away the sleep from my face and groin, trying to figure out why there was no message or data, the phone 911ed me again. Heart and respiration rates back to near normal, I dialed the Alley offices.

"Jesus, Q, don't you ever sleep?"

"I'm an avid napper, Jake." Q's voice was void of his usual surliness and disdain. "The Baron's come back out of his lair."

"Great," I growled with sleep still caught in my throat. "Where?"

"Right where you thought it would be. The West Bank near Columbus and River."

"You got an A-VIN on the synthoid?"

"Yes. I do."

"Great send me the coordinates."

"No. Get a pen and write them down so they can't be hacked."

"Right. Good thinking." I reached into the nightstand and pulled out paper and pen. Old school.

Q dictated the synthoid's chassis identification number and the GPS latitude and longitude.

I confirmed the information in a read back and started shifting gears to spur myself into action and get down to the Flats with EC.

"Hey, Jake…"

"What?"

"I was actually able to decode some of the data payload…"

Q usually wasn't so dramatic, but there was something in his voice I had never heard before: fear. "Q, what is it? I gotta get going."

"I did an extraction on the facial recognition targeting mask. I'm sending that to you now. Look at it."

My phone dinged. I looked at the screen. "Are you sure?"

"Bytes don't lie, Jake. It's her. Maddie's the next vic."

Q was right. The composite image on the screen was a dead ringer for her. "Where is she right now?"

"The I/O board and the grid show her up at her desk in Robbery/Homicide."

"No doubt still doing paperwork on that homeless guy they nabbed." I was painfully alert. "Who else knows? Did you tell EC?"

"Nobody else. I didn't want this leaking out of the messaging servers."

"You get down the alley to the House and keep her there. No matter what. And message EC to get his ass into the Flats. I'm not going to wait to meet up with him."

"Right, Jake, but what should I tell her?"

"I don't know. She definitely won't want to hear any of this."

"You know I won't be able to make her stay."

"Tell her you found something suspicious with her kid sister's credit activity or something. Do a quick search and pull something out of your ass. Just keep her there in the House. If she knows what's really going on, she'll want to jump into the deep end."

"I…Okay, Jake. I'll figure something out."

"Just keep her safe in the House."

"Right."

After a quick birdbath, I strapped up and grabbed my "Go" bag. I'd take the Department sedan. I could put it into chauf mode to enter the data Q gave me as it navigated me to the West Bank.

Halfway there, I got a call from EC. "Jake."

"What?"

"Q said she's not there."

"What do you mean she's not there?"

"He said her *iNode* has been hacked and ghosted. According to the desk sergeant, she left sometime after midnight."

"Get there. Get there now."

"Right, Jake."

I killed Rochester, went cherry top and hit eighty down the Shoreway towards the Flats.

~~~

Off the Grid

I killed the lights and siren after I blasted through the West 25th Street exit and hit the hill down the Superior Viaduct, descending into the Flats, descending into my own personal hell, praying I would find a serial killer synthoid before he found my girlfriend.

I slammed on the brakes at Center Street to take the corner without squealing the tires, then crept towards the swing bridge to the East Bank. I manually turned off the headlights. The hybrid went all electric and I silently prowled into the dark blocks like a cat hunting in the night.

"Damn," I exhaled and slammed on the brakes. *The EMI from the traction motors.*

The synthoid's sensors were no doubt tuned to detect intruders across all bandwidths—heat, light, auditory and radio frequency. If I spooked him, he might bolt into the night…or he might hurry to finish the job.

Q's ping coordinates blinked on the dash map at Lockwood and Columbus, on the other side of the river. I'd have to go the rest of the way on foot.

The street was lined with junkers and delivery trucks parked for the night. I slid the *Interceptor* in behind a step van in the space next to a fire hydrant. Before I powered down, I glassed up and pinned the locations of Maddie's crime scenes to its map. EC's techie ways would have been helpful just then, but I didn't have time to wait for the cavalry to show up. I powered down my *iNode* and tossed it on the passenger seat, along with my shield with its RFID chip. To hunt the hunter, I'd have to go completely off the grid, too.

My mind thrashed with unpleasant scenarios, wondering if Maddie was really in the Flats—but she'd have to be or why else would the data payload for her assassination hit the AnSub down here? And just blocks away from her crime scenes. Why did she come back? An arrest had been made. The city was made safe again—or so it had been told by the brass at the press conference. Some doubt must have struck a nerve in Maddie like a cavity gone bad to bring her down into the Flats in the middle of the night to revisit her victims' murders. And I knew exactly the crime scene where she'd be: the alley where her case and mine crossed paths.

It wasn't until I got to the river and reflexively checked my six that I saw the pools of light cast by the street lamps. I was living the nightmare that Q's call woke me from less than an hour ago.

I stepped out on the swing bridge, its ironwork casting shadows in the moonlight like a holographic spider web as I crossed the river.

On the East Bank, I pressed myself to the facade of an empty storefront and scanned the street ahead. There was no sign of a department sedan anywhere around the entrance to the alleyway two blocks down.

I unholstered my *eM&P* and slid forward in the shadows.

A rodent rustled down the sidewalk, hugging close to the building, unseen like me, I hoped. Second thoughts scurried like rats in my mind. I should have tried to warn Maddie by text—but no; since the Baron had clipped and cloaked her data stream, it would have only alerted him that we were on to him and nearby to help. Maybe I should wait for EC. Maybe…

Shoe leather shuffling softly on pavement scratched the quiet night from the alley up ahead. I stopped and squatted down behind the back fender of a grimy Chevy *Volt* with historic plates on the opposite side of the street. I watched the alley entrance, enhanced in eerie thermal black and white detail on my *Google Glass*.

Maddie emerged from the alley and leaned against the wall looking in, contemplating the crime scene. Her curvy body was still a half silhouette.

I unconsciously grit my teeth, gnawing the dilemma I faced. I could warn her now and save her in this moment. But the Baron's drone would still be out there, loitering in the crowd, waiting with cold and infinite machine patience to execute the implanted code, when I wouldn't be there—when no one would be there to stop it. Or I could bait the trap with Maddie.

I stayed behind the fender and watched. She'd hold it against me but wouldn't hesitate to do the same…maybe.

I manually opened up the pulse bandwidth on my *eM&P*—there'd be no time to scan for the optimal frequency—then waited.

Time just stopped. It could have been sixty seconds. It could have been an hour. Sirens from up above spilled down from the city into the Flats. Maddie looked up over her shoulder at the lighted skyscrapers. It could have been an armed robbery in progress—or any number of other crimes that warrant a Code 3 response.

Somehow I knew, though, it was EC riding to the rescue but sure to foil my ambush in the process.

Maddie surveyed the murder scene again and pushed her shoulder off the wall. She took a step back into the alley. My glass suddenly flared up with a sharp glint, a street light caught on mirrored metal at just the right angle to explode off my lenses. When the blossom of light faded like a firework, I caught the thermal shadows of Maddie being pushed hard into the alley.

I bolted from behind the Chevy and dashed across the street.

The angle was right to keep me out of the synthoid's rearward vision, but I could see him grab her jacket and lift her off the ground, feet frantically, futilely trying to find traction in the air.

The synthoid twisted Maddie like a baton and tossed her ahead, arms and legs flailing as she tumbled deeper into the alley, followed relentlessly by the Personal Services Assistant now programmed to be her murderer.

I took a deep breath, exhaled halfway, then spun around the corner to the alleyway. I double tapped the droid with my Smith and Wesson. In the interminable wait for the chamber charging sequence, I could only observe the synthoid was merely slowed in his advance on Maddie, who was crabwalking back from one mechanical fist raised above to strike down and crush her skull and the other clutching a large butcher knife to finish the inherited killer's signature.

I watched helplessly as the gap between human and machine closed, fighting the instinct to pull the trigger again too soon and send weakened EMP rounds that wouldn't stop the assault.

The synthoid's fist began to fall.

My *eM&P* shuddered against my palm and flashed green in my glass.

I pulled the trigger once, then again.

The cumulative effect finally locked the fist in midfall.

The alley was a frozen film *noir* scene in my glass. A panicked *femme fatal.* A serial killer. Sirens growing louder in the background.

The synthoid began thrashing spastically. The butcher knife clattered to the pavement. The droid finally collapsed in a heap.

Maddie's hyperventilating swelled slowly in my ears.

I let out the last of my own held breath, then inhaled deeply.

The acrid odor of ozone told me the synthoid's circuitry had been fried, so there would be nothing for Bob or Puff or Q to find.

I went to Maddie and held her in my arms as the street outside the alley filled with the noise of police cars arriving at the scene of a crime, after the fact, as usual.

Crash and Burn

"Idiot!" Puff erupted like an angry Vesuvius, spewing a hot lava flow of obscenities until he sputtered into insensibility and dove back into the synthoid's innards.

I just stood there and took it…deservedly, but Maddie was safe. Scraped, scratched and bruised a bit, but alive. Also, unfortunately, just as livid with me as Puff. About telling Jamal things I shouldn't have. About throwing a huge monkey wrench into her case. About using her like I did to be Munchausen bait. About…

"Yup, yup, yup," Bob muttered, shaking his head. It's a fish fry inside there. "Nothin' left but ash and bones. Ash and bones…"

"We'll tell Q," EC said with a heavy sigh, giving me a sympathetic sideways glance.

We pushed out a side exit on the House into the alley—Exit Alley—and slowly walked back to our offices.

"Wow. I think it's official now. You've got the whole world mad at you."

"The *whole* world?"

"Well, not me…*yet.*" EC grinned a bit. "But I'm sure I could come up with a reason or two. *If* you want to do a thorough job of it."

"Yeah…Well…"

Up ahead, Q waited for us under the unblinking surveillance camera, watching us approach like a wary alley cat.

"There was nothing," EC sighed wearily. "Zero. Zip. Nada."

"I wouldn't exactly say nothing," Q replied cryptically. "Hey, Jake, sorry about Maddie."

I shrugged. "Collateral damage. Comes with the turf sometimes."

"I mean—I couldn't help it. You know how she is. She made me show her."

"Show her what?" I asked.

"And what do you mean you wouldn't say exactly nothing?" EC growled.

Q tapped the screen of his phone and turned it towards us so we could watch a synthoid-eye video of Maddie's attack. "She made me show her. I—I…"

I shuddered at the panic on Maddie's face and the brute terror in her screaming which never registered in my ears that night. And in just how close I'd come to really losing Maddie—to the morgue.

"Jesus. What the—"

"My bloodhound code caught the stream before Jake zapped it."

"Well, I guess that explains a thing or two." I looked away from the video.

"We'll get this guy, Jake. We'll get him." EC's voice dripped with anger.

"Funny thing about the feed." Q pocketed his phone. "It split. One terminated into the Baron's *iNode* so he could watch it live—"

"That'll close the deal on a warrant," EC interrupted. "That and the money trail."

"What money trail?" Q asked.

"I finally found how Dr. Mullaney paid for the hit on her hubby. She laundered it through the Clinic with purchase orders for lab supplies to an LLC the guy owned," EC explained. "Can you put a BOLO lock on Atlas for him? We don't want him to get away."

"Sure."

I hit pause on the video replay of Maddie's attack running in my mind. "What was funny about the feed?"

"It split. Like I said, one feed went to the Baron's phone. The other disappeared into the darknet."

"What does that mean?"

"I don't know for sure," Q said with concern.

"Was he archiving it?" EC asked.

"Maybe…" Q looked directly at me. "Or someone else was watching."

"Who?"

"It's the darknet, Jake. Nobody good."

"Don't lose this guy," EC warned.

"I won't." Q looked at me one last time and muttered over his shoulder as he went inside, "Sorry about Maddie."

Yeah. Me, too.

~~~

Paperwork

Sometimes the wheels of justice move slowly…and sometimes not so much. While EC and I waited on the paperwork mill in the prosecutor's office, Maddie's perp was quickly deemed legally incompetent, which officially closed her serial killer case without the inconvenience of a trial. At least the poor sap who took the fall in the media got the mental health services he needed. Our off-the-books shadow investigation stayed in the shadows and off the books. The brass tidied up by declaring the assault on Maddie to be a PSA malfunction, not malware. And without any evidence to the contrary from Puff, Bob or Q, it stuck.

Deep down, though, she knew. She was too good of a detective. It was just another one of those situations that bureaucracies don't handle very well: too messy with too many loose ends and too much potential for radioactive media fall out—the kind that causes career cancer. Maddie knew the game. But that didn't help heal things between us.

Anyway, the city was officially deemed safe from a serial killer and everyone moved on…except for me, EC and the Baron.

Of course, Jeffery stopped showing up for work at the Clinic and the VA, but Q had a DDB—Digital Denver Boot—on him, so he wasn't going anywhere while we waited on the paperwork. Neither was Dr. Mullaney.

~ ~ ~

The Darknet

Maddie's call came through at three AM. Of course, I had changed her ringtone.

"Jesus. Why does crime always have to happen in the middle of the night," Amy complained hoarsely, then rolled over away from me and hugged her pillow.

"Yeah?" I answered, trying to be as discreet as possible.

"You're going to want to see this," Maddie said matter-of-factly. "I'll send you the details while you drag yourself out of…when you're on the way."

"Right."

Maddie was on familiar turf: The Flats.

I crossed beneath the crime scene tape and walked towards her standing guard over the covered body, holding the bunny suit crew at bay from their forensic harvest.

She nodded to the Medical Examiner to pull back the sheet from the body. "Looks like your case is closed, too."

Jeffery's corpse lay on the pavement. "But…he didn't do that to himself."

Maddie peered up into the dark night sky. "You don't have to say it, but you will, won't you? You can't help yourself."

I didn't answer. I just stared at the eviscerated body that was the object of our arrest warrant with his intestines wrapped around his neck like a fine silk tie. The only thought

that floated up in my mind was the darknet.
  "What did you call him? The Baron?"
  I nodded.
  "I guess he's still out there."
  The darknet...

*****~~~*****

Thank you for reading my story.

About M.T. Bass

M.T. Bass lives, writes, flies and plays music in Mudcat Falls, USA.

www.mtbass.net

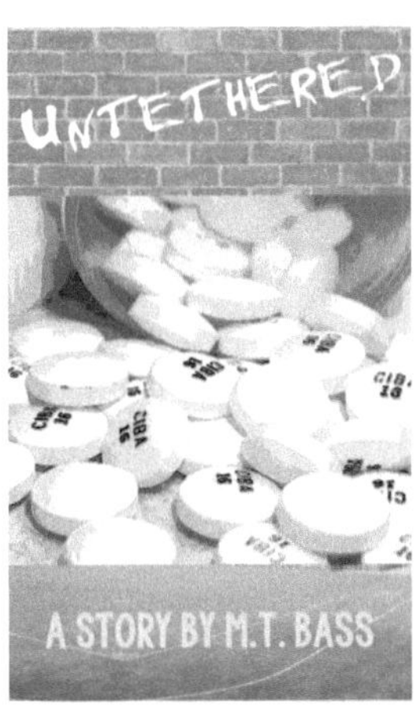

Available in eBook

At District High School #6241, Connor wants only to get close to Liz, the cheerleader whose locker is just across the hall, and forget the suicide of his father in jail, but his family's dark past and a rebellious nature force him to the fringes of student social circles and into an unlikely alliance to fight back against a tyranny of conformity.

www.MTBass.net

Available in Paperback & eBook

Anchorage, 1976 — Albert and Waxy flunk their Intro to Philosophy midterm and drunkenly decide to drop out of *The Ohio State University* and go to Alaska to "strike it rich" working on the Trans-Alaska Pipeline. After Albert's father cuts off his credit card, they get bartending & dishwashing jobs at an Anchorage bar, where Albert becomes involved with the bar owner's girlfriend, CiCi, who is also the lead singer in the house band. Albert "acquires" a union card to get a pipeline job for himself, but then learns that Waxy has become part of a crazy scheme with Jimmi the Pilot, Beantown Bob and Moe the Eskimo to find and recover a long lost government payroll from an Air Force cargo plane that crashed in the Alaska Mountain Range decades ago.

www.MTBass.net

Available in eBook

*Lodging — bending of the stalk of a plant (stalk lodging)
or the entire plant (root lodging)*

While World War II engulfs every nation on the globe, Rebecca and her high school friend Sarah can only dream of escaping a dreary, wind-blown existence in western Kansas, until their boring, stodgy old hometown fills with handsome young men learning to fly Army Air Corps bombers known as *Liberators*, and their lives are suddenly filled with temptation and, perhaps, true love.

www.MTBass.net

Available in Paperback & eBook

Kansas City, 1965 — Y.T. Erp, Jr. can't wait to leave for college at the University of California, Berkeley to escape not only the work, but especially all the phlegm-brained idiots at his father's aerospace company. Leaving behind a pregnant auburn-haired cheerleader, a sensuous red-headed siren plotting to usurp his familial ties, and his two best friends—one who ends up in Vietnam and the other in the Weather Underground—his "trip" on the wild side of the Generation Gap takes him from the psychedelic scene of Haight-Ashbury to the F.B.I.'s Ten Most Wanted list. Meanwhile, his father is consumed by the task of managing his unmanageable corporate team in the quest to help fulfill a President's challenge to "land a man on the moon."

www.MTBass.net

Available in eBook

Cleveland, 1977 — Grappling with a foreign policy crisis, the U.S. Government targets a hapless rock-'n'-roller as a Russian spy in a classic case of mistaken identity for an innocent, 'Wrong Man' hero…or *is he?* Think of an unholy fictional union between the Rolling Stones and Alfred Hitchcock's *North by Northwest*. Unlike any novel you have ever read, this one has a soundtrack. After all, a story whose characters are musicians should have…well…*music*. Right?

www.MTBass.net